Jill and the Prize Winners

by Jemma Spark

© 2022

Book Ten of Jemma Spark's Jill Series

Epona Publishing

www.ponybookuniverse.com

Trade paperback ISBN 978-0-6450263-9-9

Jill Books

Jill Rides Cross Country (Jill Series Book 1)

Jill Has Two Horses (Jill Series Book 2)

Jill Goes Pony Trekking (Jill Series Book 3)

Jill and the Mystery of the Missing Horse (Jill Short Story)

Jill and the Steeplechaser (Jill Series Book 4)

Jill Dreams of a Dressage Horse (Jill Series Book 5)

Jill and the Horsemasters (Jill Series Book 6)

All Change at Blainstock Stables (Jill Series Book 7)

Jill's Ponies: Black Boy and Rapide (Jill Series Book 8)

The Adventures of Jill's Ponies (Jill Series Book 9)

Jill and the Prize Winners (Jill Series Book10)

The Jill Crewe Miscellany No. One

Jill and the Wild Horses (Jill Series Book 11)

Dedicated to Ruby Ferguson,
Josephine Pullein Thompson,
Diana Pullein Thompson,
and Monica Edwards,
whose excellent pony books have inspired me.

Table of Contents

PART ONE
by Charles Ravenscroft

Chapter One

I hadn't wanted to write about my leg. My wretched, dragging leg. I hated how it ruled my life as if it were an entity in itself. I had had polio several years ago and ended up with a limp; what my mother had unconvincingly declared was a *distinguished* limp.

This watershed event in my childhood resulted in me taking up riding, taught by Claire at a riding school in Eastbridge. I bought my beautiful grey mare, Secret. Even as a raw novice, with the help of Claire, I had managed to compete in Foxhunter showjumping competitions. I had even qualified for Wembley in that first season but had chosen not to go. Secret and I were still too inexperienced.

Eventually, I returned to school, and I was miles behind. I was supposed to devote myself to my education to catch up with my peers. Then I entered the competition in the magazine *Riding*. The first round of prize winners was to go to Blainstock Castle in the Scottish Highlands with, or without, their own horse, for two weeks. They would compete in several different competitions, and the winner was awarded the grand prize, a weekend for two, at the Spanish Riding School in Vienna. The original competition was to write about what riding meant to you. Thus, I had written about my leg, learning to ride, Secret and my passion for showjumping.

I had no idea I would win and should have the opportunity to go to Scotland. I told my parents, expecting they would say that schoolwork should be my priority, but again they came up trumps. They said it was a brilliant opportunity, and it was the Easter holidays anyway so I wouldn't miss too much school, and you were only young once, and Mummy thought that a weekend in Vienna would be rather fun and if I won she would accompany me.

The magazine organised that Secret and I would be picked up and taken to Scotland in a horsebox. Mummy packed me an enormous food hamper. It was a long trip. I had never been to Scotland and envisaged purple moors, huge mountains, deer with impressive antlers and people wearing kilts.

We arrived at dusk, and the castle (it was a castle!) was outlined against an impressive Highland sky, full of dark, sinister clouds. Although I knew what to expect, more or less, it was a shock. This was no chocolate box scene but something huge, magnificent and medieval.

The stables, situated outside the castle walls, were equally impressive. A modern complex with an indoor riding school. This place was the stuff of dreams!

I led Secret down the ramp, and she was relieved to be on solid ground again. She looked around curiously, staring at the horses' heads hanging over the stable doors. There were small ponies, middle-sized ponies, and horses. A glorious collection of equines!

A man, Hugh Gillis, hurried forward and introduced himself and shook my hand.

"Welcome to Blainstock. You're the first of the prize winners to arrive. The others are coming tomorrow," he explained. "We'll put your mare in this loose box down here. She'll be stabled next to the other horses coming up for these two weeks. When you're not riding her, there's a wee field over there that she can go in during the day if the weather is good. It's unpredictable up here, the weather."

Secret seemed satisfied with her living conditions. She walked around, sniffed at the thick bed of golden straw, dipped her muzzle in the bucket of fresh, cold water and pulled a shred of hay out of the well-stuffed hay net.

"Linda, my wife, will take you over to the castle and introduce you to Mrs Micheldever. She's in charge of sleeping arrangements," he told me.

I liked him. He seemed very capable, and the way he spoke of his wife, Linda, with such a tone of pride, impressed me. Linda was much younger than him. Tall, slender with long dark hair.

"How long have you been married?" I asked, intrigued by this unlikely couple. She looked surprised at such a personal question. Mummy had drummed into me that I should not ask intrusive, impolite questions, but my curiosity was insatiable. I was at the age when human relationships were at the fore of my mind.

"We married about three months ago, just after Christmas," she replied.

"Is your husband the stable manager?" I asked.

"He was, for many years, but things have changed now. Hugh, me, John, previously the groom, and Jill, the daughter of Mrs Micheldever, are now equal partners in the Blainstock Stables. We've been trying to build up the new business. That's how we got to be a prize in the *Riding* competition. We're promoting the stables and also the castle, hoping for more paying guests who come up not just for the shooting in the autumn but for riding or an experience of the Highlands."

Then it struck me. I knew that the name Blainstock had a familiar ring about it. Jill, the daughter of Mrs Micheldever, was the famous Jill Crewe who had written all those books. Fiction and reality were merging as we approached the castle, a formidable structure looming out of the dark.

"Do you also live in the castle?" I asked.

—

"No, Hugh and I have our own cottage near the stables," she replied. "But John does. He's got rooms out the back, near the kitchen."

"What a wonderful place to live! Is Jill here this fortnight?" I asked.

"She's due back from Australia any day," said Linda. "She's been over there on a showjumping tour."

"What an amazing life," I commented.

"She's a lively one," agreed Linda.

Mrs Micheldever was very kind but somewhat distracted. She had a young toddler, appropriately called Hamish, and he was tugging at her skirt, demanding attention.

"Hamish, give me a minute," she cried. "Charles isn't it," She turned to me and smiled. "You're the first of our prize winners, so you can have your pick of the guest rooms. Please come with me."

She dumped the noisy boy in a playpen, calling for someone to keep an eye on him, and we climbed a curving staircase to the next floor and followed labyrinthine corridors to come upon a row of doors painted in different colours.

"We've colour coded so people can remember which is theirs," she explained. "Personally, I like the red room. A magnificent view of the moors stretches out on this side of the castle. Or from the blue room, you can see the stables."

"I'll take the blue room," I said, thinking I could keep an eye on my beloved Secret.

"Dinner is at seven. We dine early here. There's a castle map on the bedside table, so you don't get lost," said Mrs Micheldever.

"I don't want to end up in the dungeons," I said lightly. She smiled at me kindly. I was probably the hundredth guest to make such a joke.

After she left, I opened my suitcase, hung my jackets and trousers in the large wardrobe, and placed my thick woollen jerseys and underclothes in the dresser's drawers. I had brought my badges that showed my membership of the BSJA (British Show Jumping Association) and the pony club and decided that as my father wasn't around to criticise, I would wear them proudly. At home, he had complained and I had been forced to hide them under my lapel like an American special agent.

There was an hour before dinner, so I decided to dash over to the stables to check on Secret. She had looked interested and contented when I had left her, but I reasoned that it would be all very strange for her, and I wanted to set my mind at rest. I

---

had packed a flashlight and took it with me as it was very black outside. I tried to remember the way to the stables. I followed the map and made my way down some corridors to a wooden door decorated with metal studs that led outside into the large courtyard at the front of the castle. Then, there was a track to the wall with a small personnel door. I let myself through and followed the path that led to the stables.

Secret was munching on her hay net and took not the slightest notice of me. I slipped into her loose box and put my arms around her neck for a moment. I needed some reassurance in this strange place. I hadn't been away from home in years, except, of course, when I had spent those months in hospital when I had had poliomyelitis. I know that I should have been more self-confident at nearly eighteen years old, but since my illness, I have developed all sorts of minor complexes. My doting parents were worried that I had become solitary and peculiar, but I found it hard to meet new people with my wonky leg. For some reason, I felt extremely awkward trying to explain to them what had happened to me.

When I learned that I was one of those chosen to participate in this round of the competition, I received a letter from the magazine outlining the schedule for these two weeks: a mixture of instruction, competitions and fun activities. I hoped that the instruction would be of the sort approved by Claire, my teacher at the riding school. When I had first bought Secret home, influenced by my coven of cousins, loud and annoying Patience, Prudence and Jackie, I had got muddled and tried all sorts of different styles of riding. Secret had begun to rush around with her head in the air, and it had all been a disaster.

I had returned to Claire at the riding school, and she had set me firmly back on the right track, and now I was a devotee of the

Continental seat, with my feet beneath me, not stuck out in front, short reins and most importantly, at all times, keeping Secret on the bit.

Dinner that night was informal, and I was disappointed to see that neither Mr Micheldever, nor Linda and Hugh were present. Tentatively, I raised the question of what sort of instruction we would be receiving.

"I'm not sure of the programme, but Linda usually takes charge of that. She had her own riding school, you know. Before she married Hugh and brought her horses here. Of course, Jill is involved, too, when she is at home. Linda learned a lot about dressage when she was living in Germany, and I believe she is very good. We're so lucky to have her and Hugh," Mrs Micheldever replied.

I turned my attention back to my plate of lamb stew with a hearty serving of boiled potatoes and thought about this. Dressage in Germany sounded impressive, and I couldn't imagine Linda adopting the ghastly style of riding that my cousins used with their feet stuck out in front of them, sitting back in the saddle with long reins and their hands in their stomachs. But, even if Linda did instruct us in a style I knew Claire would disapprove of, I hoped that I would have sufficient strength of character to withstand the wrong advice.

I limped up to bed that night. My leg was aching. The long journey in the horsebox had caused it to cramp up. I did some exercises in my bedroom and went to sleep. The rest of the prize winners arrived tomorrow, and I hoped they would be good company.

I went down for breakfast early the next morning. There was an air of expectation, and people were rushing about, from here to there. Tentatively, I helped myself to some scrambled eggs and fried tomatoes from the sideboard and sat down to eat. Although people smiled at me and there were scattered good mornings, I sensed there was much to be done, and I tried not to get in the way.

Mrs Micheldever came dashing in and sat down next to me.

"Charles, dear," she began and paused. I wasn't sure that I liked being addressed as 'dear', but she was a sweet, well-meaning woman, and I took it in good part. "We've got a lot to do today, settling the other prize winners. Hugh suggested that you might like to go on a ride with John. Get a glimpse of our glorious countryside before we get started on the schedule. If you don't think your mare is up to it, we would be happy to lend you a horse."

I didn't need to think about it. I could imagine nothing better than getting out and exploring this wild countryside.

"I'm sure Secret would enjoy it after being cooped up in that horsebox for so many hours," I replied.

I had got it spot on. Secret was full of beans and jiggling around the yard. John held her while I mounted from the mounting block. We rode out of the stable yard. He was riding a 16 hh gelding called Shadow. He told me that the dam of this impressive gelding was a Highland cross thoroughbred mare named Bonnie, who had been bred with a Premium stallion. Somehow, Shadow had been overlooked and left in a field for years and had only been brought in and broken a few months ago. He was good to ride but still learning to balance himself with a rider's weight, and if I didn't mind, it would be a long, quiet hack.

"That sounds just the ticket," I replied. "He's certainly a good-looking horse."

"We've got his full-brother here as well. He's called Balius, and he belongs to Jill. She broke him in herself and has competed with him. He's a bit taller and perhaps a bit plainer to look at."

12

I told him about Secret and how I had bought her as an eleven-year-old in poor condition and had been training her for over a year now. I talked about showjumping and competing in Foxhunter events. John listened attentively but didn't seem to share my obsession with the sport. He was certainly a good rider. Claire would have approved of his position and strong seat.

"Look up there on the moors," said John pointing away in the distance as we walked up a path between small stone-walled fields where different horses grazed in the spring sunlight. "There's the first of the heather coming into bloom. You know there are three main types of heather: cross-leaved, bell and ling. The red grouse adore the stuff, eat it, shelter in it, nest in it, and raise their young. We have grouse shooting on the moors in August and September. That's the main part of the business. But now things have changed, and we're working on putting the stables themselves on a business-like footing, with riding lessons and equestrian events."

By now, we had left the fields behind and were riding around a loch that looked exactly how I might have imagined such a thing. The water was obviously deep, with a stiff breeze making ripples run across the surface. Just looking around at this landscape was an invigorating experience. I felt as if I were absorbing the beauty and magnificence of it all.

Then we turned off onto a narrow track.

"If you follow this path, it will take you all the way to the edge of the land, and I'm sure, if the weather holds, the whole bunch of you will spend a day riding to the sea," said John. "But today, that's too far, and I thought we might head up north for a bit."

The path was narrow and winding, and Secret fell in behind Shadow, content for him to lead the way.

We came to a rough part of the moors and stopped at the top of a hill to look down at an intricate maze of bogs and heather, rock and peat that was threaded by the meandering crisscrossing paths used by the sheep and rabbits. We continued along the path, descending into a small, hidden glen that nestled in the fold of a hill. There was a spring and rushing burn, fringed by the green shoots of fern.

"This is just like something described by the poets," I cried, but I couldn't think of exactly which poets might have written verse about Scotland. My literary knowledge was sketchy.

"Those gorse bushes will be bursting with golden buds soon," commented John

"It will be beautiful then," I said politely. I tried to imagine living up here with all this wild beauty, so different to the orderly green fields and civilised hamlets of Oxfordshire. I realised then how small my horizons were. Beyond holidays to the seaside and visits to distant relatives in London, I had never really travelled. First, there was my illness, then my all-absorbing passion for showjumping. Now, I began to see a huge, big world out there, waiting to be explored.

We rode in manly silence, and I imagined not only winning more Foxhunters but going on to jump in Grade A and then shortlisting for the British Olympic team. I added some flourishes to these well-practised dreams and went sightseeing in the foreign cities where I would be showjumping. I would visit the great museums and art galleries of Europe.

Lately, my parents had started wittering on about me becoming horse-mad, saying I should widen my horizons. I would tell them about my plans. I resolved to buckle down and apply myself to studying French more conscientiously. Anyway, here I was! Seeing the Highlands for the first time, travelling beyond my small circle of existence.

We came to a ruined stone building. I asked John whether it had been a small castle, perhaps belonging to some feudal lord. He didn't know. The track was twisting and turning now, with little hillocks, dips and crags. The sky suddenly clouded over, and the sunlight was gone. The dark high-flying clouds threatened rain.

"Perhaps we'd best turn for home," said John. "The weather can get bad up here in a minute."

I was happy to do this. Suddenly, I shivered at the strange wildness of it all. As soon as the path levelled out, John suggested that we trot. The horses were keen to return to the stables. They must have sensed that bad weather was coming.

I was glad I was with John, who knew this country very well. I would have hated to be out exploring on my own. I was relieved when the loch came into view. We were nearly back, and I suddenly wanted to be seated beside a comforting fire drinking tea and eating scones with jam and cream.

The rain began to pelt down as we entered the stable yard. John told me to run to the castle, and he would see to the horses. I trusted him now. He was a solid chap, and Secret was happy to be led away. I wasn't really much of a runner these days, but I hopped along back around the path into the courtyard and up to the front entrance of the castle.

———

Chapter Two

My leg was playing up as I limped into the hallway and stumbled into a group of newcomers. This must be the other prize winners, and I had made the most embarrassing entrance possible. My hair was plastered to my head and I was panting with the effort of moving quickly along on my wonky leg.

"I say, old chap, are you alright?" asked one young man with fair hair and a concerned expression.

"I'm fine," I retorted, feeling myself going red.

"Charles, Charles. Let me introduce you to everyone," said Mrs Micheldever. Her attempt to gloss over my limp was apparent, and my face was burning. By now, it would be an unattractive crimson hue. "I know, let's all proceed to the library for tea, and we can get to know each other."

"I'll just go upstairs to change," I muttered and, making a considerable effort, climbed the curving stairs, hanging onto the bannister rail tightly, willing my leg to work properly in front of this group of strangers.

"Come on! Come on!" called Mrs Micheldever. "Let's go to the library. I want you all to meet my husband, Richard, and there are Cook's scones fresh out of the oven and other delicious treats. We could all do with a nice cup of tea."

I got lost trying to reach my room. It was an inauspicious start to a fortnight with five strangers. All my fear and shame of limping washed back over me. After wandering down a corridor with unpainted doors and back again, I finally found the guest rooms. I opened the blue door and flung myself onto the bed in despair. So much for all my grand daydreams. I was incapable of introducing myself and performing the most banal social niceties.

Sunk in gloom, I realised not turning up for tea would make me look even more peculiar. I had to rise above it. I pulled off my dirty riding clothes and washed in the handbasin. I found a pair of decent trousers and a clean shirt. I decided not to wear a tie, made sure my badges were pinned to the lapel of my coat, brushed down my hair, pulled myself together and went back downstairs. I felt as if I were facing a firing squad.

Mrs Micheldever didn't cry out my name as I slunk through the door. She was a decent woman and had divined my discomfiture. I sidled around the room, found myself a vacant armchair, and sank into it. Then, I realised that to help myself to a cup of tea and a plate of food. I would have to struggle out of the chair and totter towards the table. I felt like screaming in anguish. Who would have thought the simple act of having tea would be so fraught with difficulties?

Mr Micheldever, who seemed as kind and considerate as his wife, materialised in front of me.

"Don't get up, lad," he said kindly, handing me a cup of tea and a plate heaped with fluffy scones, a large pat of golden butter and a spoonful of something red and jammy.

"I'm Richard Micheldever, and you must be Charles Ravenscroft," he said, pulling up a stool to sit beside me. "I'm sorry I wasn't at dinner last night, but I dined with our solicitor at Kilkarny. That's the nearest big village to us. We do have a tiny village, Craigie, with a general store and a pub about two miles away. At some point, you'll probably ride down there."

He continued to chat with a range of pleasantries that needed no more response than a nod of my head, and I stuffed some scones into my mouth. Food gave me strength, and I raised my eyes from my plate and looked around at the prize winners, who were a lively bunch sitting close to the fire and chattering.

As I was polishing off the last scone on my plate, my mouth full, one of the group got up and came over and introduced herself.

"Hello, you must be Charles with the wonderful showjumper Secret," she announced. "I saw you jumping at Haddenum. I do love your mare. She is so sweet!"

Of course, it had to be Haddenum where she had seen me! I had come fourth in the local class with four faults and had done a magnificent clear round in the Foxhunter but hadn't ridden through the finish and got disqualified. I remembered how my cousins had reacted so predictably, calling me senseless and decrying the waste of an entry fee and the cost of the horsebox.

Making a huge effort to be polite and practise at least the minimum of social graces, I replied, "Were you riding there?"

"Yes, I was on my Anglo-Arab Tranquil, like his name, he really is tranquil, the sweetest kindest horse. Of course, I didn't train him myself. My friend Noel Kettering did most of the hard work. By the way, my name is Susan, Susan Barington-Brown. I'm not even sure how I made it as a prize winner. Mummy saw the competition in *Riding* and insisted that I enter. I'm not good at English at all. I never get any of the literary allusions that people make, but I just dashed off something about how I liked being friends with the other pony club members. I belong to West Barsetshire Pony Club and some other stuff I can't even remember. I was astonished to see that I had been picked."

She was rattling on, and I stared at her. Not a great beauty, but there was something so attractive about her face. She was kind, and gentle and giggled a lot.

She was the opposite of my cousins, who were dominating, screeching and demanding. With her long fair hair, she looked like a Nordic goddess, although Nordic goddesses were rather out of fashion after the war. To my astonishment, I fell in love, tumbling down into a mysterious abyss, terrifying but compelling. This extraordinary feeling, like drinking too much wine, was entirely different from how I felt about Claire at the riding school, who was much older than me. I respected Claire, trusted her, and thought she was brilliant, but this was a different kettle of fish. I felt like I could tell this young woman anything, and she would smile in her friendly, accepting fashion and make a funny comment. But, at the same time, I wanted to be a gallant hero and impress her mightily.

"Lettie!" she called, apparently oblivious to the cataclysmic emotion sweeping through me. "Do come and meet Charles, he has the sweetest mare, Secret, and they showjump. This is Lettie Lonsdale. I'm sorry, I can't remember your surname."

"Charles Ravenscroft," I said as I struggled out of the armchair to shake Lettie by the hand. She was a thin girl with a pixie face and long, light brown hair. She looked younger than Susan and not so outgoing. I wondered if all girls and young women I met in the future would immediately be measured up against Susan.

"Lettie has a lovely bay mare called Martini," said Susan confidingly. "She's good at dressage and jumping, and she was taught by Pierre St Denise, a famous French horseman."

I was very impressed by this and wondered how I had found myself in such a group. Linda had learnt dressage in Germany, and now one of the prize winners had been trained by a European master. My fears that the instruction would be at the level of Colonel Darcy, the previous instructor at our local pony club, entirely dissipated, and I became worried that as a relative newcomer to the noble pursuit of equestrian excellence, I was going to be out of my depth.

"How did you get taught by a Frenchman?" I asked curiously.

"He's a friend of my father, and we spent a summer there at his place near Fontainebleau. I rode his little grey mare called Chiffon."

"I adore that name - Chiffon," remarked Susan.

"As it is our first night, we're having a rather grand dinner, and there will be Highland dancing afterwards," announced Mr Micheldever. My heart sank. There was no way I would be able to frolic around with Highland dancing, leaping over

swords and flinging my legs about. I had feared that my riding was not going to be up to scratch. Dancing was totally out of the question.

"My dancing teacher says that I'm the most uncoordinated student she has ever had the bad fortune to come upon," whispered Susan, giggling.

I felt a rush of love for her. Somehow, this gorgeous young woman had the power to say the right thing every time.

"We can watch together," I said in a manly fashion, resisting the temptation to touch her arm.

"We should all congregate in the drawing-room at seven for drinks," said Mr Micheldever.

"Let's go to the stables now and check on the horses. I want to make sure that Tranquil has settled down. I think he is in the next door loose box to your Secret. They're going to be great friends," said Susan.

I marvelled at how her mind ran along the same lines as mine. I sincerely hoped that Secret was not going to take a dislike to Tranquil. That would make my vision of Susan and I riding together into the sunset, side by side, extremely awkward.

PART TWO
by Lettie Lonsdale

Chapter Three

The formal dinner announcement on our first night sent my spirits plummeting. I went through the clothes I had brought, took out my best dress and tried it on. Somehow, I seemed to have shot up like a bean pole. The hemline was above my knees. I looked like a kid. All I needed were short white socks and button-up shoes. I have to admit that I *was* a kid, just turned fourteen years old. I realised that everyone else was much older, more grownup, and the girls would all be tricked out in long, elegant dresses. I was painfully aware that I was the youngest one here. I was riding Martini, my pony, only 14.2 hh, while the other prize winners' horses were at least 15.1 hh or higher. I just didn't fit in and wished that I had never come.

In my entry to the competition, I had written about my desire to train horses, to improve them. This was what I had done with Martini after she had been well and truly messed up, first by Pippa Cox, who was a timid girl who had frozen with fear when Martini had bolted while out hunting. Then, she had been sold to the ghastly Lydia Pike, an extremely unattractive young woman, well known as a pot-hunting showjumper, who practised some very dubious training methods, such as rapping. She was also known for beating her horses, whipping them around the legs, on the poll and punching them in the face. At Stringwell Show, Martini had grown so frenzied and wild in reaction to Lydia's treatment that she had crashed through the course, then jumped out of the ring, over the ropes and two rows of empty chairs. After that, Lydia advertised her for sale. We went to look at her but couldn't afford the £60 price. Then at Stringwell Market, we managed to buy her for only 32 guineas.

It had taken me ages to quieten Martini so that she could relax when being ridden. We had to go back to basics, walking over one pole on the ground for hours. She had begun to improve, and I wondered who had first broken her in.

Mummy found Mr and Mrs Cox's phone number in the telephone directory and had rung them and asked from whom they had purchased Martini. They had been rather huffy at first and said Martini was a bolter and should never have been sold to a child like their Pippa. However, Mummy was very tactful, and when Mr Cox ran out of steam, she asked who were these dreadful people who had sold them Martini. He told her Guy Beaumont.

In this way, we learned more about Martini's history. The Beaumonts had bred her, and she had been broken in by their son, Guy. They invited us over and showed us her dam, Sherry, who had been a brilliant pony hunter with perfect manners. When she had been permanently lamed, they had bred her with a stallion called Rascal of Rapallo. They described Maurice, who had helped their son, Guy, with the breaking in. Maurice had attended dressage and showjumping courses under a Continental instructor and proved himself in dressage competitions.

They were happy that Martini had eventually found a good home. The sort of home that she deserved. We invited them over for Sunday lunch. Guy was away in the army, but they promised that he would visit when he was next on leave. They told us more about what had happened with Pippa Cox. She had seemed like a good rider, sitting neatly on Martini in the field, trotting and cantering in circles. Whispers had spread back to them about how Martini had gotten the upper hand, and Pippa had been run away with in the hunting field. Too late, they had contacted the Coxes to offer to repurchase her at the price they had paid, but she had already been sold to Lydia Pyke. After that, they hadn't heard anything. They looked appalled when I told them about Stringwell Show.

"But she was such a promising young mare," lamented Mrs Beaumont. "Thank goodness. She's now in your capable hands. If you want to sell her, promise that you will give us first refusal. We never want to hear about the disasters that happened to her again."

We solemnly promised we would let them know if we decided to sell her. Although, I thought it was unlikely. If Nicholas, my younger brother, didn't want her when I grew out of her, I planned to breed from her. She was one of the family now.

I had competed at a pony club show, and we had done rather well. We had come second in an Equitation class and also second in the jumping after knocking down the stile, which had been a very flimsy jump. As a consequence of our performance at this show, I had the offer of being trained by Peter Venten, the Belgian who had written *The Training of Mount and Man*. He was teaching a few of us for the Pony Club Inter-Branch Competition at the end of the year. At this event, I came fourth in the individual class. Poor old Miss Fipps, our Pony Club Instructor, had been dumbfounded at this. She had no faith in dressage, which she thought was full of crazy notions such as leaning forward to go downhill and bothering about angles, flexions and cadence.

This had been a rather long and involved story, and it had taken me ages to summarise it in a readable form for my entry in the *Riding* competition. I must have done something right because I had been chosen as a prize winner.

It was ironic that retraining Martini with all the struggles and despair had not been as daunting as the prospect of going down to dinner wearing my

---

little girl outfit. I wondered if I could cry off with a headache, but that would be so feeble. I felt cold and sick. Then I rallied. How could I ever jump Martini in the Children's Open Jumping at White City if I was afraid to go to a dinner party? I gathered some shreds of courage and tried to pull myself together.

There was a tap on my door. It was Mrs Micheldever.

"I was just wondering if you have everything you need, dear," she said, smiling at me.

"Look at my dress," I said in despair, "it's just not right."

She looked at me.

"How old are you?"

"I'm only fourteen. The others are so much older. I didn't even think that there would be a formal dinner party," I said helplessly. "I just can't go down wearing this!"

"No, I quite see the problem," she mused. "But the solution is simple. We will find something of Jill's for you to wear. I have kept all her clothes for years now. I was thinking of doing a sort out and sending some things off to the next village jumble sale. I'm sure we can find something for you to wear. In fact, I think we might be able to fix you up with a whole new wardrobe."

I felt like Cinderella, whose fairy godmother was rescuing her.

"I *shall* go to the ball!" I whispered to myself, following her down the passageway and along several corridors. Then, like something truly out of a fairy tale, we went up a circular stone staircase to a perfectly round room. There was a massive bed, and the walls were hung with tapestries.

"Now what have we here!" declared Mrs Micheldever flinging open the doors of a large wardrobe. She rustled through the dresses that were hanging there.

"I remember when she wore this to my wedding. That is my second wedding," she explained with a quiet smile.

I hopped around on one foot, wondering if there would be anything in there that would fit me.

"This! I remember this! She was sixteen when she wore this, beside herself with excitement. She and Ann were always trying to look older. Heavens knows why!"

She pulled out a dark blue shift, long and straight with a very quiet, understated elegance.

"This should be about mid-calf level, not full length. You're still too young to wear a full-length dress. I know that there was a jacket, a dinky little jacket that gave it more oomph, as we used to say."

She rustled through the clothes hanging on the rail and triumphantly pulled out a soft grey, slightly woolly jacket with three-quarter length sleeves.

"Try these on, dear. Let's make sure they fit, but I think they will, perhaps a little big but better than too tight. Those shoes will look just fine with this outfit."

She turned away and began rummaging through the dresser's top drawer while I changed. She was so discreet. I could have hugged her and wept.

The dress was a little loose, but with the jacket over the top, this wasn't noticeable.

"Are you sure that Jill won't mind?" I asked anxiously.

"Of course not, dear. She would be happy to help. You know she's going to be back this week. I'm not sure of the day," said Mrs Micheldever.

"Someone said she has been to Australia?" I said hesitantly.

"Yes, that's right. She's been showjumping, travelling with some friends."

"She certainly has an exciting life," I said politely.

"Come on, Lettie. We'd better go down. It's time to meet the others," she replied, smiling gently but with a hint of worry in her eyes.

Drinks in the drawing room, which had seemed such a nightmare, turned out to be rather fun. It was amazing how the right clothes set you up in any situation.

"Lettie, come here and listen to this story that Patrick is telling!" called Susan.

With a glass of lemonade in my hand, I walked over and joined the group. A tall young man with fair hair called Patrick was telling a funny story about a boy at boarding school named, for some unknown reason, Bidge Major. It was a world away from my life. My little brother, Nicholas and I attended the local schools. I sipped on my lemonade, smiled, and laughed in the right places, copying Susan.

We trooped into the dining room, and it was so grand, there were nameplates at each setting. I found myself sitting at the end of the table next to Mr Micheldever, opposite a quiet young woman called Rennie and beside Hugh, who had helped me settle Martini in her loose box when I first arrived.

"Linda has drawn up a schedule of the events we're going to run," he told me.

"We'll talk to you all after dinner in the library. Announce the first small competition," said Mr Micheldever. "I must say it is rather original, the way it has been designed, so the best riders with the best horses won't necessarily win. It's a test of various skills so we can have a somewhat level playing field."

"How many of the prize winners have brought their own horses?" I asked.

"Well, you have Martini, Charles Ravenscroft has his mare Secret, Susan Barington-Brown has brought Tranquil, and Patrick has Scarlet Pimpernel," said Hugh. "The two others, Janet and Rennie, are riding Blainstock's horses."

"How many horses do you have in your stables?" I asked Hugh.

"There's the riding school ponies and horses that Linda brought from her establishment. Then Jill has three horses, Balius, a beautiful Highland cross thoroughbred, Copperplate, an accomplished little showjumper and Skydiver, a highly-trained dressage horse. Then there are three young ex-racehorses that Linda and I are planning on re-educating, and we have one three-day eventing horse, Firestorm, who used to belong to Mark Lansdowne, and there's also Shadow, who is a full brother to Balius. We thought we might try Janet on Firestorm, and Rennie can have Copperplate. Shadow is still a novice and not suitable for the sort of riding we'll be doing."

"So many horses!" I exclaimed.

The woman called Janet Fawley was sitting beside Rennie.

"I'm sorry, but I just caught what you said. I might be riding Firestorm. Is he that huge chestnut, at least 17 hh that I saw your wife riding when I arrived today?"

"Yes, that's right," said Hugh. "By all accounts, you're an experienced rider, and he's a magnificent beast. But he will also be a challenge."

"Don't worry, I'm up for it," replied Janet.

"What is Copperplate like?" asked Rennie hesitantly. She hadn't talked much, and I thought she was as shy as I was.

"She's a lovely chestnut mare, getting on a bit now, but very good at showjumping and very kind. I'm sure you'll enjoy riding her," said Hugh.

The conversation was now whizzing up and down the table, and I was trying to keep track between forking up a delicious venison stew. I suddenly wondered whether bringing Martini had been the right decision. If I had come unmounted, I would have been able to ride some of the other horses here. Then, I was flooded with guilt at my disloyalty to my own beloved pony. Not only did I adore her eager, lively personality, but the more that we did together, the better we might be prepared to do well in competitions. She had all the potential, and it was up to me to ride her to the best of my ability.

Following the venison stew, a delicious dessert was served: apple pie with a choice of custard, whipped cream, or both. I settled down to eat. Hugh, Janet and Patrick were discussing the cross-country course at Blainstock, which we were to have the opportunity to jump later in the week. I began to feel as if I were in a dream, transported to some sort of horse heaven with an indoor school, cross-country courses, and instruction, all to the backdrop of the magnificent Highland mountains and moorland. My own little world of Cherryford situated on the river Lynne, surrounded by water meadows, with our shabby-pink house with painted blue woodwork and little crooked orchard seemed tiny compared to this big world.

After dinner, we gathered in the library, and Mrs Micheldever handed out elegant cups of strong coffee. I didn't like the taste of coffee very much but was influenced by the older people here. I decided that I would try to be more sophisticated and sipped it.

Linda and Hugh stood at one end of the room and called for order. We settled down and turned to look at them. Everyone was agog, waiting for the details of the competitions.

"I want to welcome you here to Blainstock Stables," began Linda. "We have worked hard on coming up with a range of small competitions that are a little unusual, not just the normal showjumping. This is because of the basic differences between the horses you brought, the two horses supplied by us and the different sorts of riding experiences each of you has. We want to give everyone a fair chance of winning the grand prize of a weekend in Vienna."

There were smiles all around, oohing and aahing. She waited for silence again.

"The competitions will consist of jump building, bending races on the riding school ponies, each competitor doing an advanced dressage test on Skydiver, our accomplished dressage horse, putting together a double bridle in the fastest time, planning and delivering a riding lesson to our own pupils and a written test of the points of the horse."

She paused and looked around. Everyone was chattering.

"A dressage test on Skydiver!"

"Bending on ponies should be fun!"

"I'm hopeless at putting together a double bridle."

"I haven't done points of the horse since I did the pony club D test."

"I've never given a riding lesson in my life!"

"Jump building! Are we meant to be practising our carpentry skills?"

When the hub bub died down, Hugh took the floor.

"We have two well-known riding personalities coming up to judge the competition. They will be arriving on Tuesday morning. Tomorrow we'll be preparing you for some of the competitions. More explanations of the exact details of how they're going to be run will be given later."

I was sitting there deep in thought. Perhaps I would have the advantage when bending on a smaller pony as I was shorter than the other competitors. Advanced dressage on a dressage horse promised to be terrific. I had no idea about jump building. It sounded completely different to my amateur attempts at constructing jumps out of household items. I marvelled at the ingenuity the organisers had exercised. It was all going to be great fun, but I doubted that I would actually win.

"Are we going to get some instruction and jumping practice as well?" asked Patrick.

"Yes, in the mornings, there will be schooling sessions in the indoor school or the outside jumping arena, and at the weekend, when we've got our usual pupils, we thought we might let you loose on the cross-country course, organising yourselves. You'll get one schooling session on Skydiver, and you'll each do a different test on him. So, you're going to have to learn a test."

"Will we be doing any trekking?" asked Charles.

"Yes, we'll put aside a whole day and ride to the sea," replied Hugh. Mrs Micheldever will meet us down there with a

sumptuous picnic lunch. There'll be a chance to bathe if you can brave the cold water," he went on with a wry grin.

"Ooohhh," shivered Susan dramatically. "I don't think so."

"I wonder who the mystery judges are?" asked Janet. "Do you think you could give us a hint, Linda?"

"Well, one of them, their family lives nearby," said Linda with a quiet smile.

"Who lives nearby?" asked Charles.

No one answered his question, and Mrs Micheldever announced that a local group of Highland dancers had arrived, and we were to go into the hall, and they would be teaching us some dancing.

I forgot any remaining misgivings when we began to dance. We had a hilarious time. Charles Ravenscroft, who had a limp, sat out on the side lines talking to Mr Micheldever, but everyone else joined in. None of us were at all elegant or skilled when it came to dancing but it was very boisterous and jolly.

Chapter Four

At breakfast the following day, high spirits were bubbling over. It was our first morning in the indoor riding school, and we were to get some dressage instruction from Linda. Amid the excitement, as everyone tucked into porridge, scrambled eggs, fried bread, bacon and toast, in walked Jill Crewe.

For a moment, there was silence. Most of us recognised her, and there she was, as large as life, joining us at the breakfast table, introducing herself and asking us our names. I wondered if she would be just as funny and charming in real life as in her books.

"Now to horse!" she called as we rose from the table. She led the way. "I can't wait to see my horses after being away for so long!"

We arrived at the stables, and Linda, Hugh and John must have been up since dawn. All the boxes were mucked out, and the horses to be ridden this morning tacked up, ready for us. Martini was shining as if she had been groomed to within an inch of her life, and instead of luxuriating in a feeling that both of us were being waited upon, it made me uncomfortable. I would have preferred to have attended to her myself. I resolved to set my alarm for six in the morning tomorrow so I could be down at the stables looking after my own mare.

We mounted in the stable yard and walked the horses the short distance to the indoor school. Jill was riding the very tall and impressive-looking Skydiver, the famous dressage horse. I looked at this combination critically but admitted that they made a splendid picture. Skydiver was a lovely dark grey with a silken mane and thick tail. His quarters were well-developed, and you could see that he was trained correctly by his muscle structure. I was sure that Pierre St Denis could not have faulted him.

We walked around the school for at least ten minutes, loosening up the horses after they had been confined in their boxes all night. Martini was the smallest of them, but I believed she could hold her own. Although she is delicately made, she has short cannon bones, long forearms, and a well-bred and intelligent head. I had been watching the stellar career of the showjumper Stroller, only 14.1 hh and competing in all the top competitions in England and this gave me hope that Martini could also make it to the top of the sport.

Charles Ravenscroft was riding his mare Secret. She was a good-looking Anglo-Arab mare, stepping out with a long stride, looking attentively around the school, obviously very aware of her new surroundings. Susan Barington-Brown's horse, Tranquil, was also Anglo-Arab, and like Secret, 15.1 hh. True to his name, he seemed to have a very placid and kindly nature, just like his owner, who could be relied upon to chatter away pleasingly and optimistically. Patrick Huntingdon was riding a very tall bay gelding called Scarlet Pimpernel, who belonged to his friend Valerie. The horse's legs were disproportionately long for his body, but his movement was extremely graceful. His head was long and narrow and his ears large, but he walked quietly on a loose rein, and Patrick looked like a good rider.

I was particularly interested in the Blainstock horses that had been given to Janet and Rennie. Firestorm looked true to his name, although I wondered if Brimstone might not have been more apt. He was without doubt an extremely handsome horse with a huge personality. He had a long neck, which gave him an admirable length of rein when he was ridden. But, for all his good looks, he didn't look comfortable to ride. As Janet pushed him into a trot, I saw how huge and bouncy was his stride. I couldn't imagine even trying to sit to a trot on him. Quiet as a mouse, Rennie was riding the sweet Copperplate. The little mare looked like chocolate wouldn't melt in her mouth. Jill was trotting on Skydiver, and there was something so rhythmic and assured about his perfectly cadenced stride. He was obviously trained within an inch of his life.

Linda strode into the centre of the arena and asked us to canter on, and after a few rounds, she said we should do a simple change across the diagonal when changing rein. She told Jill to lead the ride. It was stipulated that we go from canter to one or three strides of walk and then strike off again. I liked this. It was something a bit different. Undoubtedly everyone could do flying changes, but this transition from walk to canter was a good exercise.

Then we were instructed to do some shoulder-in, when you walk forward with the horses' shoulder on an inside track and the quarters following an outside track.

"Can you remind us of the aids, please?" Charles asked.

Linda gave us the aids and reminded us that this movement required flexion through three separate hind leg joints. From there, we went on to do renvers, half-passage and turns on the haunches.

"Now, I'm going to get Jill to demonstrate one of the advanced dressage tests. We've chosen six tests so that Skydiver doesn't learn any of them by heart. Each of you will have to memorise a different one. You'll also each have a private lesson on Skydiver before you perform the dressage test."

—

We lined up at the end of the arena and watched Jill on Skydiver. I was hugely looking forward to having a go on this trained dressage horse and performing advanced movements. To me, it was going to be one of the high points of the fortnight. Jill and Skydiver were not of the standard that would be seen at the Spanish Riding School, but their performance was definitely magical. There was silence as we watched. No one commented or chattered, or fidgeted. We were collectively spellbound.

At lunch, the journalist from *Riding* arrived. He was a cripple, not just like Charles, but hobbling along on two sticks. He didn't seem very friendly, his face set in a grim, almost disapproving expression. I wondered what sort of article he

would write. Then the whisper went around that he had been a jump rider and had had a horrendous fall resulting in him never being able to ride again.

After lunch, we were given details of the jump-building competition. We were to work in pairs, and they had been decided for us. Undoubtedly Linda and Hugh had noticed Charles' infatuation with Susan, so playing cupid, they kindly put them together. Then there was Janet and Patrick, and I was placed with Rennie.

I was relieved as Rennie seemed even more shy and quiet than me, and I took the lead. We were given some ideas, and I thought that perhaps I could exercise my artistic abilities, such as they were. I asked Rennie how she liked the idea of painting scenery on an old wooden wall that had seen better days.

I began to sketch some ideas. On numerous occasions, I tried to paint pictures of my own house next to the river, where two swans glided up and down throughout the summer. It was the obvious choice for one side of the wall. I thought I could do the castle with the mountains in the distance on the other side. It was truly magnificent scenery up here. I wished that Mummy could have come too as she could have helped with the painting, but that was childish. It was time to grasp the paintbrush and do it myself with the help of Rennie.

We were taken to the workshop, and I investigated the range of paint colours available. There were a lot of basic colours, and I thought with some judicious mixing I would be able to get the colours that I wanted.

Rennie was enthusiastic in her quiet and understated way.

"Have you done much painting?" I asked.

"Not really," she admitted. "But I love your ideas, and I'm sure I can do a bit to help with the background colours if you do the tricky bits.

"Why didn't you bring your own horse?" I asked.

"I never owned a pony or a horse in my life," she said in surprise. "Do you think that everyone owns a horse?"

"No, I guess it was just my assumption," I replied.

"I work with horses, like Janet. We look after and ride other people's horses," she stated simply.

"We don't have staff or anything like that," I explained quickly, not wishing to seem like a spoilt miss. "My little brother Nicholas and I look after Martini, and we have a small pony called Pablo."

"Although come to think of it, my father is going to marry Miss Brandon, who owns the riding school where I work, so I guess they'll be owned by my stepmother, somebody in my family. But, you know, I never even thought of it in that way," said Rennie. Suddenly she smiled. "I just love horses and ponies and all animals. I don't think of them as possessions."

I felt embarrassed. My simple question seemed to have opened up a whole can of philosophical worms. I decided that I would take more care with my assumptions in the future.

That second night's dinner was comparatively informal. We were told to wear casual clothes, and I had an inkling that Mrs Micheldever thought of me when this was announced. After dinner, we played the sort of games that people play at country house weekends.

We started with charades which were great fun. Most people chose books, and it was interesting to see who had read what. A range of classics was chosen, like *Water Babies*, acted out by Patrick flapping his hands around like waves of water, then rocking a baby in his arms. I didn't guess any of them. I was hopeless at this sort of thing.

After charades, we went to the games room and divided into two teams for a darts match. None of us was any good at darts. The least worst was Charles, and the very worst was Rennie.

After that was a riotous game of Sardines, where one person went off to hide and as each person found them, they crammed into the same place. Jill was the first person to hide as she knew the castle well and hid in the scullery cupboard. Patrick, a systematic person, located her first and climbed in with her. Then Susan found them and joined them. Unfortunately, she was an inveterate giggler, and it wasn't long before everyone found them, and Janet was the last person.

Afterwards, we had hot chocolate in the kitchen and pigged out on Cook's sultana and nut cookies. Tomorrow the mystery judges were to arrive.

———

PART THREE
By Bevan St John

I had been a jump jockey with a promising career, and it had all been cut short by a fall that left me with two smashed legs. I had lain in hospital for months and months in agony and despair. There hadn't been enough morphine in the world to take the edge off my pain. My family had visited dutifully. My mother was worried and spoke in hushed whispers as if we were in church. My father had been bracing, telling me to buck up and recalling the injuries suffered by his friends in the war. Neither of these attitudes was of any use at all.

All my life, I had wanted to be a jump jockey. During my childhood, I had deliberately chosen not to eat too much. I didn't want to grow. Fortunately, jump jockeys don't have to be as small and light as flat racing jockeys. My father had a stable full of hunters, so I had my pick of horses on which I could practise my future profession. I had hunted every day that was possible when I wasn't away at school. I had gone to pony club, revelling in the cross-country jumping and also competing in hunter trials. My dreams were full of galloping and jumping. Speed and winning were all that I thought of.

When it became evident that I would never be able to ride again and I would be lucky if I avoided life in a wheelchair, my father began to suggest an alternative career. He talked about being a trainer, but I couldn't face it. Watching the jockeys galloping and jumping would be too hard. I couldn't bear it.

At school, I had not been up to much. I had managed to get by with the least amount of effort, sitting inconspicuously in the bottom half of the class without being a total dunce. My best subject had been English, although to be more accurate, it was my least worst. For this reason, my father had decided that I should be a writer, and he had wangled me a job at *Riding* magazine. My father was not someone who could be easily denied. He was a cardboard ogre of the hunting, shooting and fishing genus. But, when you came face to face with him, his piercing, furious blue flash of eyes was persuasive. He decided that as I couldn't bear to be sitting on the side lines of the racing world, I could still work in an equestrian field, as that was all I knew.

Riding was a magazine for horse people of all types, not mainly focused on fox-hunting and hounds like *Horse and Hound*. It was full of information about riding, pony club and all things related to stable management. At first, they had placed me in the advertising department, but I didn't feel very charming when I got out of the hospital. I was positively gloomy. Selling advertising needed more than a fraction of charm to tempt the advertisers into investing their money in our magazine, so they had hastily moved me out. I worked for a while in administration in the subscriptions department, but this had been too dull. I would spend several hours a day staring into space and dreaming of a life I would never have.

If it hadn't been for my father's influence as a close personal friend of the Editor, I'm sure that I would have been sent away to pursue an alternative career. Instead, it was decided that I wasn't cut out for sitting in an office all day, so it was better if I could be sent out into the field. I was to gather news, write it up and submit it to the sub-editors who would polish up my raw efforts, so they were fit to be published.

That is how it came about that I was sent to Blainstock Castle to report on the six prize winners who were enjoying two weeks there, competing in further competitions to decide who was to go to Vienna. I was to observe their activities and make notes. Then every evening, write it up. This whole fiasco could provide enough material for a book, and I was to capture every aspect of it. Unfortunately, they decided that it was too expensive to send a photographer with me, so I was given a crash course in taking pictures and given two rather expensive cameras with which to practise the art. They figured that if I took enough photographs, something would have to be usable.

I arrived at the castle at lunchtime on Monday. The daughter of the house Jill Crewe, had arrived this morning after an extended holiday in Australia. She was something of a celebrity. I had heard of her, vaguely through her pony books that I'd never read, but more through some articles, she had written for *Horse and Hound*. I thought she would be a stuck-up young miss who was more ego than substance. I have to admit that I regularly thought of other people in negative and cynical ways, at least ever since my accident when my life had collapsed in a miserable heap.

After this introduction to my pathetic and feeble self, I wouldn't blame you if you didn't skip to the next section, which a more uplifting and inspiring personage will undoubtedly write. I think I've been included to add some grit to the airy-fairy happy-happy people who are currently pursuing their horsey dreams. Indeed, the six young prize winners were all hopeful specimens who looked in a good position to make it to the top of their chosen sphere of equestrian endeavour if that was what they wished.

There was Susan Barington-Brown, who appeared never to have spent more than a minute of her life feeling miserable, whose father had heaped upon her every type of horsey accoutrement and the best horse flesh to indulge her in her hobby. If I were to be extremely mean, which I hope I'm not, I might have thought she was a trifle bovine in appearance as she didn't have

---

34

the refined features of a society beauty. Still, she did have a certain milkmaid charm with her big blue eyes and long blond hair, which she usually wore in plaits. A young man with a decided hobble was circling her like a shark, ready to take his first bite of delicious young flesh. I did feel some kinship with him and then learned his story. He had suffered from polio and ended up with a limpy leg. Through that experience, he had taken up horse riding rather than my own story in which riding horses had resulted in permanent disability.

Then there was Janet Fawley, the eldest of the six. She was the one who had pulled herself up by her bootstraps, or in this case, her elastic-sided jodhpur boots. She had not come from a horsey family and had been a town child born and raised in a terrace house. Yet, from an early age, she had no greater ambition than to be a perfect groom. She spent nine months as a working pupil at an urban riding school and then secured a position working for the Claude family. True to all horsey-happy-endings, she had been allowed to ride her employees' mare, came second in an important one-day event, and was offered an even better job where she was to help train horses for cross-country events. In my estimation, she was undoubtedly the most worthy of the prize winners and probably deserved to win the competition.

Little Lettie, as I thought of her, was the youngest, at just fourteen years old, and she was undoubtedly a gifted rider with a very nice little mare. I hoped her parents could give her the right opportunities, and she might well be winning national junior showjumping competitions. I hadn't had much time to investigate Patrick Huntingdon, who was riding a rather strange thin horse that looked a little distorted to me. And Rennie, she was the odd one out. Apparently, she had had some health issues. Whether they were physical or mental was unclear. She had been mounted on Blainstock's Copperplate, who was a kind-hearted little chestnut mare, who looked after her admirably.

On that first day, I sat down to lunch. They probably thought I had something to do with the judging as they seemed nervous about me. I suppose I was a representative of the magazine sponsoring this jamboree. Still, I did not have any input into the judging, so there was no need for them to shoot me covert, nervous glances.

The group had spent the morning in the indoor riding school and were being coached towards one of the competitions, in which each of them rode an advanced dressage test on Jill's horse, Skydiver. He was an out-of-this-world horse, and the chance to do some advanced dressage was causing a lot of excitement. I didn't much hold with dressage, which was part of the new-fangled European thing that was infiltrating, possibly contaminating, the good old-fashioned British riding world.

The afternoon activities sounded unutterably dull to me. The prize winners were to be given more details of the competitions. They each had a different advanced dressage test which they had to memorise. There was also another competition to be announced. I knew I should be taking numerous notes, but I wanted to stay in my room and read one of my detective novels, which was my favourite form of escapism.

My legs were encased in leather braces, and I had to walk with two sticks. I had decided that sticks were better than crutches. This made me feel very conspicuous whenever I had to move around in a crowd. Everyone looked at me with pity. They probably thought that, but for the grace of God, they had so far escaped such a fate.

Jill was different to the others with their suppositions and polite silence.

"What's wrong with your legs?" she asked when we were seated in the library, waiting for Linda to arrive with the dressage sheets to be handed out.

"I had a fall competing in a point-to-point," I explained.

"Poor you. It looks like you must be in constant pain," she commented.

"That about sums it up," I replied shortly.

"It doesn't look like you can ride again," she went on.

I wished she would shut up and leave me to my miserable self, but she was indefatigable.

"That's right. No more riding."

"But I suppose you could still take a pony out in harness," she went on. This persistent 'looking on the bright side' had to be the most irritating thing about being debilitated.

"Probably," I replied brusquely. Due to being a representative of the magazine, I had to stop short of being positively rude to the daughter of the house.

"I have to go into the village after the meeting today. The others will be embarking on preparations for their second competition. We could harness up Bonnie to the trap, and you can see some of the countryside," she went on.

I could see no way of politely declining this opportunity. Instead, I sat there with a black expression. She ignored this and told me we would leave at two-thirty this afternoon. Thus, I found myself bowling along a small road that led to Craigie less than two miles away.

"I suppose you need some background to write about the castle and what facilities are available to visitors," she prattled on. I saw this as part of the big push to get themselves more business.

"Here, you take the reins," she said and thrust them into my hands. I had no option but to steer the solid little grey cob.

"Bonnie was bred at Blainstock, you know. She's half Highland and half thoroughbred. I have one of her sons as a riding horse, and there is another full-brother, Shadow, who belongs to the riding school."

She prattled on, talking about the different horses at the stables. There seemed to be every possible permutation of horse flesh.

Perhaps driving a horse in a trap would inspire me to a new horse adventure, but nothing happened. We trundled along. I could feel Bonnie, who did seem like a decent little mare, through the reins, but it was nothing like jump racing. It was too drearily pedestrian. This was not going to be the answer to my life choice dilemma.

Desperate to move Jill on from this catalogue of equines, I asked her about her trip to Australia. I seemed to have hit a raw nerve.

"I was showjumping with a family called the Heywards. We travelled in a huge truck as far north as Cairns and then down to Victoria," she said as if reciting from a cheat sheet.

I sensed that she was holding back now. I could be as close as an oyster when questions were asked about something I didn't wish to talk about, and this was the case now with Jill. I pondered for a moment. Should I press her with some searching investigative questions but then decided that I couldn't be bothered?

We bowled into the village. A general store seemed to sell every object one could need. A family ran it called the McIvers, who had four lively children in the shop stacking the shelves. One couldn't move without falling over one of them, and I had to lean against a shelf and watch from a distance. Three children had bright-red hair, and the youngest had a mop of black curls. I gathered from the conversation that they owned a pony called Tippy, who lived at Blainstock and they regularly hired other ponies so that more than one could ride at a time.

"Great news!" said Jill cheerfully. "I've brought my old pony Black Boy up to live at Blainstock. He's a fantastic ride, just 13.2 hh and has been competing in gymkhanas forever. Next time you're up at the stables, you must have a look at him."

This news was received with great joy, and I gathered that they all knew of Black Boy from reading Jill's books. I was cringing at the horsey enthusiasm that seemed to saturate every utterance and thought of these children. I began to feel that I needed to move into a different world where no one ever thought of or mentioned a horse. Perhaps the idea that I should stay in the equestrian world was a mistake. Of course, there was nothing I could do for now. I was stuck up here for the duration, and I would keep going. If nothing else, these two weeks in my life had revealed something. I had to choose a different path.

The McIvers carried our parcels and helped to stow them into the trap. There was a lot of patting and fussing over Bonnie, a favourite.

"Canna have a drive of her?" asked the boy, Stewart.

"Surely," replied Jill. "Hop up, and you can take us out along the road a bit, but then you'll have to walk back."

She showed him how to hold the reins and make the obliging Bonnie walk and then trot when we got to the edge of the village.

Chapter Six

We returned to the castle in time for afternoon tea. I had to admit that the food in this place was delicious. You couldn't fault it. I stuffed myself with fluffy, golden scones, bright red jam, and thick clotted cream. The prize winners were chattering away, ten to the dozen, about the second competition. They were to pair up and build a showjump, something creative, and different. Of course, Charles and Susan were together. That had been a foregone conclusion. Janet and Patrick were working together, and that left Lettie and Rennie.

They huddled in pairs, sketching designs and discussing their plans in strained whispers. An air of purpose pervaded the air. Mrs Micheldever busied herself, pouring cups of tea and handing out food. Finally, she pressed me to try a slice of Dundee cake made by Cook.

Mr Micheldever sat down beside me.

"I was wondering if you might like to come out in the boat on the loch with me tomorrow," he asked.

I brightened at this suggestion, anything to escape the ubiquitous horsiness.

"I would love to," I said with an enthusiasm that surprised me. "But I have to keep taking notes of what is happening."

"Don't worry about that. Our Jill is an experienced writer, and I know she'll be happy to help. Just with notes, and then, of course, you can write them up," he replied.

I would have gladly let Jill write them up for me. Instead, every day playacting as a journalist, I realised just how unsuited I was to this profession.

"Jill, come here and talk to Bevan," called Mr Micheldever.

Jill broke away from a conversation with Linda and Hugh and came over to sit with us.

"If you like, I could have a go at typing up your notes for you," she offered. I looked at her suspiciously, wondering if she were psychic. "I don't mean to trample on your ground. I'm not trying to take over."

"No, I would appreciate any help you have to offer," I said quickly. The more time I had sailing on the loch, the better, as far as I was concerned. It occurred to me that Jill would have liked the job of writing the article for *Riding,* and this was her way of muscling in, but I didn't care. She was welcome to it, and undoubtedly she would be much better at it.

At breakfast the following day, I dressed in what I hoped were suitable sailing clothes, baggy trousers that covered my poor battered legs in their braces and a cheerful shirt.

"The judges are arriving this morning," said Jill to me in a conspiratorial whisper as we sat down to the inevitable porridge. "I know who they are, and I can write up some background on one of them. Mark Lansdowne, Richard's nephew, and his parents live on the Lansdowne estate next door. He's coming with Mercedes Pevensy." She paused as if expecting some reaction from me, but the names meant nothing. "Her family are aristocrats. She's an Hon and a pretty good three-day eventer. They live at Shrove Langton near the village of Chatton, where I lived as a child. She and Mark as a couple have been big news in Oxfordshire, and now as they're judging together, there's an angle of whether they might get married. Lots of gossip there for us horsey types."

I looked at her blankly. The imminent nuptials, or not, of a Mark Lansdowne and a Mercedes Pevensy meant absolutely nothing to me. However, the name Pevensy did sound familiar.

"That's the Duke and Duchess of Tolkington, isn't it?" I exclaimed, suddenly joining the dots.

"Yes, that's right. I've never met her, but the Duchess, Aggie, is famous as a powerhouse in the community. She has a finger in every pie. Her husband is mad about automobiles."

Suddenly she looked up like a pointer spotting prey. There was a rustle of movement at the doorway and a collective gasp from the prize winners who stared with spoons or forks midway to their mouths. It was fairly obvious that they recognised at least one of these people.

"They've just arrived," Jill gasped, with barely suppressed excitement, her eyes dancing. She had some personal investment in this power couple, but I didn't think it was pure adoration. There was an edge to her voice. Perhaps, she had been keen on this neighbour herself.

"Give us the lowdown," I said quietly. Usually, people didn't need to be asked twice before imparting scurrilous information.

"Mark dumped his former girlfriend, Diana Barton-Tompkin and set off in hot pursuit of Mercedes Pevensy just before Christmas. Her family are not only aristocrats but massively wealthy. Mark was so desperate to catch her that he was forced to go and live with the Miss Farthingtons. They're two dotty old women who live in a big falling-down house with millions of animals. They had a horse living in their dining room, and Mark had to keep his own two eventing horses in the dining room as well."

"Couldn't he have afforded to put his horses in a livery stable?" I asked in surprise.

"No, the family trust got burgled just before this, and the lawyer ran off with all the money of the Lansdowne family and our family," replied Jill nonchalantly. "That's why we've got the prize winners here. It's a marketing ploy to put Blainstock Stables on the map and attract more customers."

"So, that means you and Mark Lansdowne are related?"

"Only by marriage," she said stoutly. "My step-father is his uncle."

I nodded. It was beginning to make sense.

Jill jumped up. It was the first time I'd seen her addressing the group. Perhaps she had decided to assert her authority.

"Good morning, Mercedes and Mark. Let me introduce you to the prize winners. This is Mercedes Pevensy, a well-known three-day eventer and Mark Lansdowne."

I found this interesting. From my understanding, they were both well-known three-day eventers, but Jill had deliberately only given the title to Mercedes. I saw Mark flash her a poisonous look. Then he averted his eyes. Jill then went around the table introducing each of the prize winners, and myself, who was described as a journalist from *Riding*. Once upon a time, I would have been a jump race jockey.

Mercedes Pevensy, the Honourable, was indeed a cool and aristocratic beauty. She had a cloud of dark hair, a perfect complexion and the serene expression of a Madonna. She was exceedingly polite and correct. I wondered what lay beneath this polished surface. Mark was more interesting. He was decidedly handsome with a thin hooked nose and curling nostrils. He held his head high and looked down his nose at those around him. There was an air of arrogance about him. He was not someone I would go to for help.

The couple sat down and drank coffee, chatting politely with the prize winners. I wondered how close they were to each other. If Mercedes was staying with Mark's parents, then that signalled that they were an item. I did remember her mother then. Aggie Pevensy, the Duchess of Tolkington, was well known. I think that my father had mentioned her a few times. I could almost claim, although it might be somewhat tenuous, that they were family friends.

I hadn't been going to hang around for long, but Mercedes had finished her coffee and made her way down the table, displaying impeccable social manners. It was my turn for her attention. She looked at me questioningly. Wondering how I fitted in.

"Good morning," I said on my best behaviour. "I'm Bevan St John. I believe my father, James St John is friends with your parents. He's a hunting and fishing chap."

"James St John," echoed Mercedes. "Oh yes, I do remember meeting him once. How do you do? What are you up to here?"

"I'm the journalist sent up by *Riding*."

"Oh! That's interesting. How long have you been working for the magazine?" she asked.

"For about a year now, first in advertising, then subscriptions and now field journalist," I replied wryly.

"I see you're gaining experience in all areas, no doubt aiming to be the Editor one day," she replied lightly.

I looked at her admiringly. She was so polished, so smooth, and even with it I sensed that she was genuinely kind and interested. What a divine woman! Then, I became aware of the hostile gaze of Mark Lansdowne. Mercedes saw my eyes slide towards her paramour.

"Mark Lansdowne, let me introduce you to Bevan St John. He is the journalist from *Riding*."

There was nothing warm or charming in Mark's voice when he said, 'how do you do'? Instead, he shot me a cold laser glance. I smiled at him in a lively manner, ignoring his frostiness. This man was going to be too easy to tease.

After that exciting exchange, I didn't hang around for further observations. I would leave Jill to produce a written account of the new arrivals. I was off to go sailing. Of everyone here, it was Richard Micheldever who I liked the best. There was something extremely decent about him. If ever I needed someone to talk to, which I didn't! He would be the one.

According to Richard, the sailing boat was fourteen feet long and gaff-rigged. There was a stiff breeze blowing that morning which he said was an ideal condition for sailing. He taught me how to tack, and throwing yourself from one side of the boat to

the other was awkward, but I had developed quite a bit of strength in my torso and arms so that I could manage it without too much difficulty. The technicalities of the ropes, the sails, and the rudder were not hard to grasp, but the feeling of whizzing across the top of the waves, of being at one and at the same time master of nature, was what thrilled me. I felt a vitality that I had not experienced since my last race, which, I have to add, I had won by several lengths on a very good horse called Monkey Mins.

Mr Micheldever had asked me to call him Richard, which was a relief, as 'Micheldever' is a mouthful.

"That's not a Scottish name, is it?" I asked.

"You're right, although the family have been here for several generations. My great-grandfather lived in Jersey originally, then he moved up here and bought the old castle, which he restored, stone by stone. It's taken a while for the locals to accept us, and there's still a whiff of the attitude that we're incomers. Of course, my sister married Major Lansdowne, who is very British, and that hasn't helped with becoming Scottish."

We strolled back to the castle for dinner. My legs played up hellishly, and I had to lean heavily on my two sticks.

"I hope it hasn't been too much for you, old man," Richard said tactfully.

"Not at all. I loved it!" I replied with such a note of happiness and positivity in my voice that I surprised myself with my new mood.

Dinner that night was not a relaxed and jolly affair. Jill had offered to take photographs for me. She said she had to polish up her photography skills as she had taken a few pictures for the articles she had written for *Horse and Hound*. I noticed that Hugh, Linda and John were absent. They were probably exhausted from all the organisation that went into the daily activities and more than happy to miss out on the strain of making polite conversation.

Now I am using a nautical metaphor that befitted my new passion in life. They had rowed the boat out with the dinner setting, and there were little tartan flourishes with some very Scottish table ornaments. The best silver flatware must have been polished up, and candles all around the sconces in the wall, lighting up the rather gruesome animal heads with their glassy eyes staring down at us.

Mark and Mercedes were sitting side by side in the middle of the table with Richard at the head and his wife at the foot. Mercedes eclipsed every woman in the room, wearing a deep claret coloured dress that showed off her ivory white skin and dark hair beautifully. It had a deep décolleté which was artfully concealed by six strings of tiny jet beads. It even had a short train and full sleeves that reminded one of an imperial Chinese robe. It looked perfect in the setting of the medieval room and everyone else paled into insignificance. I was not one to go chasing after women but I felt an unaccustomed stirring in my loins.

Staff, who were dressed up in black and white with tartan sashes, were carrying in food. There were five courses, and the cook had excelled herself. I made a mental note to talk up the food in my article.

There must have been some grouse stored in the freezer, and it was served as the main meal. I had been told about the shooting every August and September, and this would be a way to include it in my article. I found myself seated down the tail of the table near Mrs Micheldever, between Janet and Susan, opposite Mercedes and Jill. These five females were going to have to share my masculine attention.

Janet was wearing a decent taffeta dress with a blue design on a background of white. It was not couture like Susan's but well-cut and simple. For all its obvious high price tag, Susan's dress didn't sit well on her. I decided it must have been chosen by her mother or elder sister, who she had told me thought of nothing but house decoration and furnishings. Perhaps, they had decided to decorate Susan as a table lamp.

Charles was seated at the top of the table, next to Richard Micheldever, and I could feel him glowering at me. He was but a boy, and he would have to learn to be more sophisticated when pursuing a love interest. Lettie was seated on his left, and opposite was Rennie.

The most interesting people at the dinner were Mark and Mercedes. They were undoubtedly a handsome couple. Seated opposite Mercedes, I had plenty of opportunities to admire her understated English rose beauty. It was hard to identify her feelings towards Mark. She was so assiduously polite that she didn't display non-verbal clues about her feelings. I deduced from what Jill had told me that Mark had been pursuing her determinedly from the first moment he had met her. I had learned that his family were now on their uppers, and his private income had disappeared over the horizon with the dishonest lawyer. Mercedes' family was not only aristocratic, but they were wealthy. It would be facile to assume that Mark was merely after her money. The way he looked at her showed much more than that. He was easy to read. She was the cypher.

I knew from my experience yesterday that Jill was a chatterbox. I could hear her interrogating Mercedes about her horses and the events in which she had competed. Janet was listening in, drinking in every detail to add to her store of knowledge of the higher echelons of the equestrian world. Susan was having a very relaxed conversation with Mrs Micheldever, telling her about the West Barsetshire Pony Club. I could see Richard manfully tackling a conversation with Rennie, who was a fish out of water. Patrick was discussing the finer points of training horses with Lettie. Looking down on this dinner as if I were hovering above it, I was struck by so many young people all teetering on the edge of adult life, eager and excited about the endless possibilities laid out before them.

I had been like that before my accident, and now I felt a hundred years old. But today had been good. I had decided that I would get my father to buy me a small yacht, and I was going to set sail around the world. It didn't for

44

one moment occur to me that this might be an equally dangerous activity as jump racing, but that was probably the reason that I was drawn to it. It was not entirely unrealistic that I should end up as a ragged piece of flotsam in towering gale-driven seas, but my head was full of dreams of freedom, skimming around the oceans of the world. I would relish the solitude and escape the pitying glances that I constantly encountered.

PART FOUR
by Janet Fawley

Chapter Seven

I saw what Bevan St John had written about me in his chapter, and he had described me as 'worthy'. Somehow, this didn't seem like a compliment. On the contrary, it suggested someone rather dull, and perhaps being of lower middle class, or even working-class origins, I had somehow done well for my type of person.

I was glad that Bevan, who was not a happy soul, hadn't known that I was a Red Cross Cadet at school and when I had worked for the Claudes, I had joined the Goatly-in-the-Marsh detachment to have an outside interest and meet people. Bevan might have interpreted this as the epitome of a 'worthy do-gooder'. Instead, it would be more accurate to say that I was gregarious by nature and working with animals all day did not do a lot for my social life. That was how I had met Tanya Miller, who was a very vivacious and entertaining young woman. Her mother was Russian, her father was English, and she had a hunter called Minuet.

When it was first suggested that I meet Tanya, Miriam, one of the Claude daughters, had declared that she was 'not my type'. I'm beginning to wonder exactly what it is about me that leads people to make such judgements. Do I give the appearance of worthiness and stodginess? If I'm not careful, I might start getting a complex of some sort!

I must admit when I first met Tanya, she was very attractive, stylish and glamorous, and I did think that she was too sophisticated to be interested in me. She was living at home for a year before she was to go off to Paris to study art. However, she was charming, relaxed and friendly and became a good friend. Tanya's hunter, Minuet, was a dark bay mare, about 15.1 hh, with a finely cut head and large eyes.

Because Miriam Claude had broken her arm, I had been put up on Corrymeela to ride in a one-day event, and we had come second. Consequently, I had been offered a job by the Thorneycrofts, not as a groom but as a rider who would help train the horses across country and do some basic dressage. Mr Thorneycroft was a possibility for the British Olympic team. The Claudes had persuaded me to accept the job, and I had gone to my new position with high hopes.

There had been a few bumps in the road along the way. The other grooms, who also rode the horses, had looked at me with an instinctive antagonism that I suspect is often the plight of a new staff member, especially when working in a highly competitive environment. I had often thought back wistfully to when I had worked for the Claudes, who had been very kind and welcomed me into their family life as if I were an equal.

At the Thorneycrofts, I ride at least four horses a day and have had several falls over fixed cross-country jumps. I feared that I might lose my nerve, but somehow I remained steady. One of the male grooms asked me out, and I accepted. This caused a huge hullaballoo as one of the female grooms had had her eye on him, and she saw me as an interloper who was stealing her boyfriend. I was totally confused by this sort of catfighting and withdrew in a hurry and no longer addressed even a single word to any of the men who worked there.

Next, a very unkind and untrue rumour was circulating that I was being over-friendly with Mr Thorneycroft. This would not only have been unprofessional but seeing as he was married to a delightful woman I liked very much, it was soul-destroying.

Mrs Thorneycroft had found me sobbing in my room and coaxed the whole story out of me. She declared that she knew it was untrue, that her husband's feelings for me were not romantic, and she believed me when I told her I would never pursue a married man. I said it would be best if I left, but she declared certainly not, I was the most promising rider they had ever employed, and they were not going to lose me. I don't

know what she did, but from then on, none of the staff said a nasty word to me. But nor did they say anything friendly either. I was finding it very lonely being sent to Coventry.

Going to Blainstock Castle had been more than just an opportunity for two weeks of fun in the Scottish Highlands. It would give me a reprieve from the stress of my job at the Thorneycrofts. I had to decide whether it was worth staying with them or returning to a more menial position as a groom. I guess I had to weigh how important a congenial work environment is compared to good prospects as a competitive rider.

On Tuesday morning, I did my dressage test on Skydiver. I had ridden several well-schooled horses in my riding life, but he was something else. I revelled in the controlled power of his paces, his gracious acceptance of the bit that came from good schooling and no lack of spirit on his part. Linda Gillis was an excellent teacher. Her experience in Germany stood her in good stead, and I thought there was probably no better dressage instructor in the United Kingdom, or none I had ever heard of.

The night before, I had memorised the dressage test I was to perform, and I declined to use a prompter. It couldn't have gone better as we floated through a series of advanced movements. I could take no credit for this. It was all down to this extraordinary horse which must be one in a million. Experiencing such advanced expertise would be a baseline for my future efforts at schooling horses. Linda explained that in England, they train horses and riders from the beginning, but in Germany, they put beginner riders on advanced horses, so they can experience what they aim for. I was determined to remember every movement and its execution.

Tuesday afternoon was devoted to our jump-building activity. I was working with Patrick, who was a decent chap. He deferred to my ideas and was exceedingly polite. The two other pairs were engaged in much more ambitious projects. Neither

Patrick nor I were very artistic and had resorted to a classic hogsback with some interesting fill in the middle. It was the best we could come up with. With such a simple design, we did not need to go to the carpentry workshop where Susan and Charles had taken up residence. We would have time to do it later. We would paint some flat boards with an intricate geometric design of six different colours. Hopefully, this would pass muster.

"They must be building themselves a house and stable complex in there," quipped Patrick, in a rare moment when a light-hearted comment broke through his reserve.

We decided that we should go for a ride around the loch. It was a beautiful afternoon, cold but bright with a light breeze that brought the smell of freshly bloomed heather wafting down the hill slopes. It would have been easier if I could have ridden any other horse in the stable, but for some reason, I had been designated the extremely challenging Firestorm.

I wondered why I had been given this monster of a horse and thought that they might have overestimated my riding abilities. He was a huge gelding with an impressive physique. I had learned something of his history, and before Blainstock Stables had taken him on, he had been one of Mark Lansdowne's eventing horses and had had a dramatic fall at Burghley. When I had ridden him in the school, he was like a tightly coiled spring, his skin twitching, his mouth chewing nervously at the bit. Now that I had experienced the sheer delight of riding Skydiver, I wondered if I could help curb Firestorm's rebellious streak but decided it was probably beyond me.

Patrick was riding the rather peculiar thin-faced and thin-bodied horse that belonged to his friend Valerie. I think it was the only time he became talkative when he spoke about this girl with whom he was infatuated. I hoped for his sake that she returned his feelings, or he was due to go through a youthful experience of unrequited love from which he might never recover.

I looked around at the Highland countryside as we walked side by side. On this rare occasion, I felt like I could relax a little on Firestorm, who seemed content to blob alongside Scarlet Pimpernel, soothed by the grandeur of the scenery. In the far distance, majestic peaks were etched against the sky. On the slopes of the hills that rose from the side of the loch were black-faced sheep that watched us curiously as we rode past. A curlew was drifting in the sky above us.

Mentally, I compared this with home. Not North Oxfordshire where I now lived, but the streets of Manchester where I had been brought up; the smell of the big city, the lamp light, the gas works, the ceaseless roar of traffic, the lights and activity of the railway station, the flashing of signals on the lines, the burning dark glow of the engines' fires, the smooth pavements and civilised gutters that carried away the rainwater that some days fell as if it would never stop.

I felt as if I had come a long way. My parents had held up my friends from school as examples of what could have been my life. Mary was earning £6 a week working at Freeman's. She was doing very well for herself. But here I was, mixing with all types of interesting people, seeing the world on horseback and learning new things. I felt contented. After doing that dressage test this morning, I was sure I was on the right track in choosing a horsey life rather than a secretary working in the city.

"Shall we trot on, do you mind?" asked Patrick, as always prepared to defer to my wishes.

"Certainly," I replied, putting my deep thoughts aside and paying attention to Firestorm. I had to keep him on the bit and balanced at any pace faster than a walk. It was an understatement to say he was a handful. There was something odd about this horse. He didn't seem to be wired in the ordinary equine way.

That night was a grand dinner, and I wore my only best dress, which I had also worn on Sunday night. I was seated next to

Bevan St John, who seemed to enjoy causing little waves of trouble around the place. I guessed that he was bitter about not being able to ride anymore.

I enjoyed watching Mark Lansdowne and Mercedes Pevensy. With any luck riding the Thorneycrofts' horses might mean that I would be competing one day against them. It was an exciting thought, and sitting here in the banqueting hall of a castle, it seemed that my dreams might one day come true. If only things at the Thorneycrofts' would improve when I got back.

Chapter Eight

I descended the stairs early for breakfast. I was used to getting up very early. Three of the other prize winners had already come down, Charles and Susan, who were becoming inseparable, and Patrick.

"Good morning, you four," said Jill cheerfully, striding into the room. "Patrick, it's your dressage test this morning."

"Oh, Patrick are you looking forward to it?" asked Susan, who seemed to be in a continual good mood, no matter what. "I'm sure I'll make a complete muck when it's my turn. Everything seems to go in one ear and out the other with me."

"But you know you've had years of pony club instruction by Major Holbrooke," said Charles fondly. "You'll have absolutely no excuse not to do well."

"My best friends, Noel Kettering and Henry Thornton, they're fantastic at dressage, and I know I'll never be up to their standard," she explained. "Anyway, Charles, you're the one who has won a Foxhunter competition. Dressage will be a breeze for you."

"I do have the advantage of having been taught by Claire," admitted Charles. "But showjumping is what I love, and flat work is just the necessary foundation for my passion. I did think we might have a showjumping competition in some form or another."

"I think they decided that the disparity in the horses' abilities would make that difficult. But I know you'll spend a lot of time this weekend on the cross-country course. Have you not thought of eventing, Charles?" suggested Jill.

"It all seems complicated to me. I'm afraid I just don't have the concentration for the dressage nor the courage to gallop downhill," he replied modestly.

"I'm sure you'd be brilliant at eventing," said Susan warmly.

When everyone had breakfasted, we dashed down to the stables. As usual, the horses were all tacked up. Scarlet Pimpernel had been let out in a small field with stone walls. Nervously, Patrick mounted the magnificent Skydiver.

Linda announced that we should go to the outside showjumping arena, and she would take Patrick on his own in the school. Today was showjumping, and I thought it would be interesting to see how Firestorm performed. He felt as if he could leap to the moon with the power in his hindquarters and magnificent physique, but only if he decided that was what he wanted.

Linda and John set up a grid for us with cavalettis. There were ten jumps, each eighteen inches high, three to four yards apart, so the horses would bounce down with no extra strides between the obstacles.

"It's difficult to set this up to suit all of you. Obviously, Martini and Copperplate will have a shorter stride than Firestorm, but I think you can all manage. Lettie and Rennie, you need to do your best to get your mounts to extend, and Janet, you can shorten up Firestorm's stride so that he is bouncing. Can you trot around the school to warm up, I think, without your stirrups, so we can do something towards strengthening your seats."

Linda wasn't going to give us an easy ride this morning. We were going to have to work hard. Firestorm was probably the most challenging horse I have ever had to ride. His stride was so long and bouncy that I found it very hard to sit to, and rising trot with no stirrups didn't make it any easier.

"You can take your stirrups back and shorten them to jumping length," called Linda. "Then canter on down the cavallettis. I watched the others go before me. Lettie had to push Martini to bound between each of the jumps, but together they did well.

Copperplate was a darling mare who looked after her rider and made it easy for Rennie. The distances between the jumps for Tranquil and Secret. I could see how Charles had done so well in Foxhunters. Secret loved jumping as much as he did, and she fizzed excitedly at the challenge. Firestorm felt as spirited as usual, and I took a firm hold on his mouth and closed my legs around him. He was a tempestuous rebellious horse, which made it strange that he responded best to an active rider who took responsibility for his way of going. It was as if he couldn't control himself and wanted someone to take a firm hand with him. We got through the grid without hitting anything, but we were almost catapulting over the jumps to get the distances correct due to his long stride.

"Now, we're going to mix it up," said Linda. She and John dragged over a pair of wings and a single pole, and with one stride from the end of the grid, they set up a three-foot jump with no groundline."

"That is rather tricky," said Susan in surprise.

"I'm sure you'll all manage very well. There's no point in not giving you a challenge," said Linda.

I decided that Firestorm would have to bounce on the spot more, and I cantered him in some small circles, sitting upright in the saddle, bringing his hocks beneath him and putting him on the bit. This time he did much better. He had realised how he had to pace himself, and he leapt the last obstacle with a foot to spare. I nearly got jumped out of the saddle, but I managed to regain my balance within a stride.

"Well done, Janet," called Linda. "Susan, you need to put more energy into your riding. Make an effort. Charles, your enthusiasm does you credit but remember you need to keep calm so that Secret doesn't get het up."

We cantered around several times.

"Alright, walk on a loose rein for five minutes to reward the horses for doing so well," said Linda. "We're just going to put up another jump. You land from the three-feet jump and turn left and do a half-circle ten yards in diameter and then three long strides, and we'll have a nice wide jump so that the horses who have been gathered together with bouncing strides then have to stretch out with some speed and extension for a wide jump."

She and John built a triple bar. It was only three feet high but quite five feet in width.

"I want you to jump once and then cross your stirrups and go over again," said Linda.

I saw Susan roll her eyes, but Charles seemed thrilled at the challenge. We all jumped clear again. Although Lettie and Martini were straining to jump wide over the triple even though they did manage the ten yard half circle well. We crossed our stirrups. I hoped I wouldn't come off. It wasn't me who fell, but Rennie lost her balance over the triple bar. I jumped off Firestorm and left him to walk around the arena, hurrying over to her lying on the ground. She had her eyes shut, and for a moment I thought she was unconscious. Her breathing was shallow. Being careful not to move her, I asked if she was alright. She opened her eyes and tentatively stretched out her legs. They were still working. Then she stretched out her arms. Gently I helped her sit up.

"Are you alright, Rennie?" asked Linda.

"Yes, yes, I think so," she replied. She sounded dazed.

"Perhaps I was asking too much of you," said Linda with concern. "Janet, would you mind helping her back to the castle, and perhaps a cup of sweet tea would help."

"Of course," I replied. "Charles, can you catch Firestorm and lead him back to the stables."

Mrs Micheldever was fussing around us, and I got the feeling she was aware that Rennie was fragile. She hadn't mentioned any special health conditions, but perhaps it was something she wouldn't want to talk about. We sat in the library and sipped tea with some biscuits to nibble on.

I kept quiet so that Rennie could relax without feeling the need to make conversation. Then, after a while, I wandered around, looking at the books on the shelves. They were real books that had been opened and read. Not brand new leather-bound editions that were merely for decoration. After some time, I heard the prize winners coming in the front door and making their way to the dining room.

"Do you want to go down to lunch, or perhaps I could bring something up?" I asked.

"No, no, I don't want to make a fuss. I feel fine now. I really do," insisted Rennie.

We went down to the dining room together.

That afternoon we were all having a go at riding the school ponies, and we were to have the bending race that was part of the series of competitions. I was looking forward to this. It promised to be great fun. Rennie stoutly declared that she would participate, and no one wanted to argue with her.

After lunch, we made our way back to the indoor school. We drew lots to see who got which pony. The choice was: Cammie, chestnut with a white blaze and white socks; Jester, a bright bay with a hogged mane; Misty, a lively grey Highland gelding; Bonnie; Peppie, a grey gelding with an ugly box-head; and Taffy, a small, ill-tempered dun gelding.

Patrick, the tallest of the prize winners, had drawn one of the smallest of the ponies, Misty. When he mounted, his feet came down to the pony's knees. I watched him ride around, and Misty was quick off the mark, more than any other riding school pony I had ever seen before. He pulled him to a stop in a single stride and then swung him around on his haunches,

spinning on a sixpence, and they set off at a gallop in the opposite direction. The pair looked like a shoo-in to win the bending race.

John and Hugh were setting up the poles. They told us we could have a practice and warm up the ponies for half an hour before the competition. I had been designated the other small pony, Taffy. It was as if I had been transported to a childhood I had never lived, flung into the midst of a pony book, galloping around in gymkhana events. Suddenly everything seemed hilarious.

"Shall we have a trial?" I called to Patrick.

We lined up, and Patrick shouted go! Misty shot off at a gallop and seemed to know exactly what to do, bending around each pole. At the end of the line, he spun so quickly that Patrick got suspended in mid-air and found himself sitting in the sawdust. My pony was not as fast, but at least I managed to stay in the saddle, so I beat him.

"You two look hilarious!" taunted Susan. She was riding the 15 hh bay gelding Jester. "I love this horse, he's only an inch shorter than Tranquil, and he is straightforward to ride. I'm going to have a go around the poles."

She lined up and set off. Jester cantered very sedately, bending correctly around each pole, an elegant half-circle at the end and back down.

"He might be easy to ride, but I don't think he's got a lot of speed," I commented.

"No, I think you're quite right. I might as well be riding Tranquil." She laughed.

Charles was mounted on a steel grey gelding called Peppy.

"This pony is very good at jumping," he said. "John told me if we had a showjumping contest, then he would be the one to win."

"And bending?" asked Janet.

"I don't think so," said Charles, "but let's see. Janet, you be the starter."

Charles and Susan lined up, and I shouted, "ready, steady, go!"

Peppy jumped and bounded in half-leaps but overshot the poles and had to be dragged back and generally misbehaved. Susan won easily, in spite of Jester's lack of speed.

"I think that Rennie and I have the prettiest ponies," said Lettie, riding Cammie a rather flashy chestnut with a wide blaze and white socks.

"John told me that Bonnie is the mother of that big grey gelding Balius, and also his full-brother Shadow. Have you seen them in the stables?" asked Rennie.

"OK, you two have a go against each other," Patrick called.

They lined up, and I said go, and off they shot.

Cammie did look very pretty. He arched his neck, flicked his tail and cantered up the line of poles. Unfortunately, his turn at the top was a disaster. Instead of pulling up and spinning on his hocks he cantered a very loopy half-circle. Bonnie did slightly better but had a rather solid body and lumbered along.

"She's very comfortable to ride," said Rennie, "her canter is like floating on a thick cloud, like a marshmallow, but I don't think bending is her best subject!"

"Ten more minutes to practise, and then you will all compete against each other," said John. There were now six lines of poles. "It will be easier than trying to do heats."

We all practised turning our ponies in a last-minute attempt to beat each other.

"I think the turn at the top is what makes it or breaks it," Patrick said. "The best way seems to pull up and swing the pony around on his haunches."

"Like a dressage turn on the haunches," I said, laughing.

"Yes, just what I did on Skydiver this morning," Patrick replied.

"I wonder what it would be like to ride Skydiver in this event?" I mused.

"It is unthinkable that such a majestic horse should be ridden in such a flippant way," Patrick replied.

"Time to go!" shouted John. "Line up. Any order that you like."

We all rode forward, and our ponies teetered along the start line.

To my shame, my bad-tempered mount lashed out at Susan's Jester, who shied away, looking shocked and put out. He was nervous now and hung back, not wanting to line up correctly. I was sent to the end of the line. Lettie was so busy watching Taffy's hind legs as she was on the other side that she missed the call to go. Patrick got a good start and was two poles ahead of everyone else. Susan's legs were going like windmills, and she was pushing Jester hard trying to make up for their slow start. Patrick and Charles were in the lead. They were neck and neck at the turn. Both executed turns on the haunches that were not elegant but effective. By now, I was just one pole behind on Taffy, and I was shouting encouragement at him. Susan was still working to keep Jester up to the mark, but he would never get past Misty and Peppy. Charles was controlling the box-headed grey admirably, and managed to keep his seat when the pony was doing this unusual leaping movement which did cover the ground swiftly.

Patrick and Charles flashed past the finish line neck and neck. I was just half a neck behind them.

John and Hugh were having a whispered conference. Then John stepped forward.

"This is our first competition with results, and I am pleased to announce first Patrick with five points, second Charles with four points, third Janet with three points, Susan with two points and Rennie with one." Lettie was last and hadn't scored any points at all. I felt a bit guilty that she had missed the start because I couldn't control my bad-tempered mount.

"Hurray! I won!" Patrick shouted, carried away with a feeling of heady victory. "I know it's only a bending race, and I don't stand a chance in the dressage or the jump design, but at least I have won one competition," he said apologetically.

He and Charles were laughing and slapping each other on the back. I smiled happily. Lettie refused to look cast down. She had come last, but she was a good loser, and at least Rennie had scored one point

PART FIVE
by Susan Barington-Brown

Chapter Nine

I'm not sure how I got to be one of the prize winners. I was just not the sort of person that ever climbed to the top of the class or came anywhere in competitions. No, that is not entirely true. I have enjoyed some success competing in gymkhanas and horse shows, first riding my expensive mare Beauty and then on Golden Wonder, who had formerly belonged to the very successful show rider, June Creswell. I know very well that this was not due to my extraordinary or even ordinary skill; it was because my father had bought me two tip-top ponies for a large amount of money. I did try hard to school my ponies and improve my riding. I was aided and abetted by my good friend Noel Kettering, who is exceedingly serious and conscientious about schooling ponies and horses and learning everything she can about equestrian matters.

Noel and I have been West Barsetshire Pony Club members for many years. We have received first-class instruction from Major Holbrooke. As well as rallies, we've had the benefit of special courses that the major has run. Henry Thornton is also a member. He is Major Holbrooke's nephew and a 'special' friend of Noel's. Everyone expects them to get married one day. I am also friends with John Manners, who I have known for years. At Pony Club Camp last summer, everyone was raving about Henry and how handsome he was. I know he and Noel are made for each other, and I flat out declared that I much preferred John Manners. I wasn't lying. I do prefer John, who is more down-to-earth than Henry, who tends to prance around like a show horse, neighing and saying clever things.

Now, here I am at Blainstock Castle. I hadn't even wanted to enter the writing competition, but Mummy had noticed it in my copy of *Riding* magazine and insisted that I write something and send it in. She is like that. She and my older sister, Valerie, are crazy about entering every competition they ever see. Particularly competitions in their favourite magazines such as *Homes and Gardens*. They share an obsession with interior decorating and are always arguing about ways our house, Basset Towers, might improve. I must admit that it is a hideous house and could certainly do with some improvements. An eccentric shipowner built it with a great deal of money and absolutely no taste. It would probably be better to raze it to the ground and start again. It is built in a ugly red brick and is too high for its length, and on each corner, there is a pepper-pot turret which makes it look absolutely ridiculous.

My mother and Valerie are always putting on airs and graces, which is a little embarrassing as my father was the son of a grocer, but through hard graft and some luck, he became a prosperous shoe manufacturer. Consequently, we went hurtling up the social scale. Now he has a chauffeur called Cookson, but he still drops his 'aitches when he talks, and there is no mistaking his humble origins. Even so, my mother and Valerie continue in their snobbish ways. My mother is tall, gaunt and acid looking, with cold fish-like hands. My sister takes after her being tall and thin with blonde hair piled in elaborate curls on top of her head, sticking out teeth and a discontented expression.

My father loves me very much and buys me anything he thinks will make me happy. He was very fond of a pony called Snowball in his youth, so he has always encouraged my interest in horses. Now, I've finished school and Mummy wants me sent to Switzerland to go to a finishing school. She thinks it will increase my chances of catching a desirable husband. I have pointed out that until Valerie marries, I should not even be 'out' as was the custom in the Jane Austen era. It wasn't me who came up with this spurious argument, but Noel, who is a dab hand when it comes to literary allusions, suggested it to me.

My mother didn't even understand the point. She was annoyed that I mentioned that no man has shown any interest in marrying Valerie so far. Daddy had waded in and insisted that I should make up my own mind about my future. This is all very well, but I am utterly clueless about what I want to do.

When I had been selected as a prize winner and was coming to Blainstock Castle, Daddy cleverly suggested that I might meet a good type of young man. I am surprised that this prediction should turn out to be true! On the day of my arrival, I met Charles Ravenscroft, and I've been in a tizzy ever since. His determined pursuit might have been overwhelming, but as we were nearly always in a group with the other prize winners, the effect of his mission to win my affections was kept at bay.

I can't wait to go home and tell Mummy and Daddy and announce that I will not need to go to Switzerland. My own home-grown charms have been sufficient. Now, I'm only seventeen years old, and Charles is also seventeen, almost eighteen, but he's still at school. How can I declare that I'm to marry a boy who is still at school? His education was delayed due to him being sick with poliomyelitis. But, he has assured me that he is set on a course to study law and hopes to go to Oxford University. He lives in North Oxford, not more than twenty miles from Bassett. How much of a coincidence is that! Obviously, we were meant to be. I can't wait to get home and tell Noel. She will be absolutely gobsmacked.

This afternoon I came fourth in the bending race, which meant I gained two points. Not a glorious beginning, but better than nothing. I was proud of

---

Charles, coming a valiant second to Patrick.

"When you put the ponies away, we'll gather in the tack room, and you'll be given your diagrams of the points of the horse that you will be tested on tonight after dinner," said John with a big grin stretched across his face.

There was a collective gasp. This was the second of the competitions. Now things were hotting up. We tended to the ponies, then waited in the tack room. The suspense was intense, and I decided to get the ball rolling while we were waiting.

"Let's start! There is the poll," I said, pointing to the top of the head on a picture of an elegant thoroughbred hanging on the wall. "Now, you have a go, Lettie."

"The wither," said Lettie, pointing to the lump at the base of the neck, in front of where a saddle might sit.

"The croup," cried Rennie jumping up, sliding her finger and pointing to a position along the horse's back that would have been behind the cantle if he had been saddled.

"I don't think it's going to be so simplistic. There's sure to be questions about certain bones and parts of the hoof. Tricky stuff," suggested Janet.

"We're going to have about three hours at the most to memorise it," said Charles.

"I can never remember anything," I groaned.

Hugh came in and handed each of us three sheets of paper. There was one with the basic points of anatomy that most of us knew. Then, there was one with different muscles labelled and another with bones.

"This is more difficult than I could have possibly imagined," I groaned again.

"I've never even learned the ordinary points of the horse," said Charles.

Janet was looking rather smug.

"In my first position as a working pupil, I had to learn all this," she crowed, "so that puts me in a good position!"

"You're just trying to psyche us out," Patrick retorted.

"I'm glad to see that the competitive spirit is alive and well!" said Jill, who appeared in the doorway. "Tea is now served in the library. So, perhaps you can get your brains working with some calorie intake."

We walked towards the castle, our eyes glued to the sheets that had been given to us.

"You'll be tested on 15 different points, five from each sheet. If that is at all helpful," said Jill.

"I don't suppose you can give us a hint?" I asked.

"If I gave you all the same hint, then it wouldn't make any difference, and if I gave it to only some of you, then that wouldn't be fair," said Jill. "So, in answer to your question, no."

We helped ourselves to tea and sat down with our eyes glued to the diagrams. Some of us were reciting the names of the different points under our breath. Charles declared that he found it easier to learn things by writing them out.

We muttered away to ourselves and to each other.

"The trachea."

"Oesophagus."

"Diaphragm."

"Kidneys."

"Elbow."

"Point of the shoulder."

"Patella."

Rennie was waving her fingers and hands around in the air.

"What are you doing?" asked Charles.

"It's a form of kinaesthetic learning," she told him. "Moving my body helps to lodge the information in my brain."

Some of the rest of us tried this method. There was a certain logic to it, but if anyone walked into the room, they might think they were in a lunatic asylum.

Dinner was a muted affair. Mrs Micheldever said that it was fine if we wanted to keep studying while we ate. The usual

etiquette of not reading during a meal would be suspended on this special occasion. My brain was starting to ache, memorising terms such as "suspensory ligament," "axillary artery", and "coccygeal artery."

"I think that you've all tried your hardest to memorise. Let's put you out of your agony," said Jill. "If you go into the library, you'll find an exam paper and a pen on each chair. You'll have thirty minutes to complete your test. Good luck!"

I rushed with the others into the library and sat down with my piece of paper. There was a diagram of a horse with blanks to be filled in with a letter. A list of all the points we had to learn and as many extras were printed on a separate piece of paper. This made it easier. If worst came to worst, we could guess. I immediately recognised five ordinary points, and I got them straight away. This gave me confidence. I took a deep breath, remembering Noel telling me that extra oxygen helps the brain work. There were two more that I thought I knew, and I wrote them in. If I changed my mind, there was room to cross out an answer and write in another. Now there were eight that had me stymied. I puzzled for about ten minutes, then lifted my head and looked around the room.

Rennie was sitting there staring into space. Either she had done it all in record time or given up. Charles was scratching his head, scribbling and writing, scratching, scribbling and writing. Janet was sitting there looking thoughtful, staring at the paper.

I decided to try doing some finger exercises. Perhaps thinking of something entirely different would help, aided by the kinaesthetic method. I went back to my piece of paper and wrote down my best guesses. There was no point straining right up until the last minute. Therein lay the path to madness.

Jill came round when the time was up and made sure that we had each written our names on our papers.

"We're going to mark them straightaway and will then announce the results. Too much apprehension is not good for anyone's blood pressure."

Mr and Mrs Micheldever came in with a tray of cups, an intricately decorated silver coffee pot, and a dish of delicious chocolates.

"You must all come and have coffee and help yourself to chocolates," she said, smiling kindly.

We compared notes as we sipped our coffee. We had each guessed entirely different things, as far as we could remember. I had blown up my brain and no longer really cared who had won this competition.

"I feel like a limp rag after that," I said, helping myself to four chocolates. "If I don't eat, I shall collapse in a puddle of helplessness."

"It's just an excuse to gorge yourself on chocolate," taunted Janet, also helping herself to four chocolates.

Mercedes and Mark came in.

"Here are our esteemed judges!" announced Jill, with a trace of sarcasm as she said the word 'esteemed'.

"I will put you out of your misery and read out the list. The winner, who scored a magnificent 15 out of 15, is Rennie Jordan, who is given five points. Well done, Rennie!"

Everyone clapped enthusiastically. No one could resent Rennie doing well. Thank goodness her fall this morning hadn't affected her brain processes.

"Second with only two mistakes is Janet Fawley, four points to Janet."

Again, there was a round of clapping. I don't think anyone was surprised by this. In fact, we had all probably thought that Janet would win.

"OK, no more clapping. I'll just reel off the other results. Patrick is third with four wrong, three points. Lettie is a close fourth with five wrong; therefore, two points and Susan is fifth with six wrong; therefore, one point."

"Oh! Charles! Poor you to come last!" I said kindly. "We'll keep each other company at the bottom of the rung."

Charles looked rather pleased with this comment which I hoped would mean a lot more to him than winning.

I was calculating where we all stood in the competition at the moment. Patrick was standing first with eight points, Janet was a close second with seven points, Rennie was third with six, Charles was four points, I was three and Lettie had only two. Patrick must have been doing the same thing as he was looking utterly thrilled.

We were all het up with so much adrenalin, coffee and chocolate, that we sat around chattering for at least an hour before we went up to bed. We didn't actually talk about the way the points were adding up, but I guess everybody had done it for themselves in their heads.

Chapter Ten

I woke the following day thinking, 'I have to do my dressage test today'. I was the third prize winner to have a go, and I must admit that I was looking forward to it. By all accounts, Skydiver is meant to be an out-of-this-world horse. Janet and Patrick have already declared that once you have ridden Skydiver, you might as well die and go to heaven.

I chose my best jodhpurs and jacket so that I looked smart. I had to lift my game. At the moment, I was sitting a dreary fifth in the competition. I had to score good marks in the dressage if I was to at least finish closer to the top. I was pretty confident that my jump building was good, but then so was Lettie's. Of course, I didn't expect to win, but I didn't want to come last either. Although if you thought about it, someone has to.

I tripped down to breakfast, thinking, 'today is the day'. I was determined that having had the benefit of Major Holbrooke's instruction for years, not to mention endless hours of schooling with Noel, there was no excuse for me not to do well. Moreover, I had spent a long time using a pencil drawing on a piece of paper to remember the test, and I was sure it was now imprinted on my brain.

Charles was down before me, and I felt him watching me the minute I walked through the door. This experience of being adored by a handsome young man was certainly very agreeable. I would recommend it to all my friends. I couldn't wait to introduce him to my chums in Oxfordshire. I knew that Noel and Henry would certainly approve of him. I was a little uncertain about John Manners's reaction, but I hoped that they would get on.

I sat down and ate a slice of toast, butter and marmalade. I didn't think I could face porridge or bacon and eggs, not today, the day of my dressage test. I sipped a cup of tea and reviewed the test movements in my mind.

The others streamed in for breakfast.

"Is there a resident ghost haunting this castle?" asked Lettie.

"Yes, I thought I heard something in the night. I woke up, but then I went back to sleep," said Patrick.

"I didn't hear a thing, slept like a log all night," said Charles dismissively.

The issue of the weird wailing in the night was passed over, and they began talking about their morning, which would focus on how to give good instruction.

"Have you done a lot of teaching?" Lettie asked Janet.

"Yes, quite a lot," replied Janet modestly.

"I've never made a single comment on anyone else's riding," said Charles. "I've had plenty of private thoughts about how my cousins ride, but I've never attempted to suggest they do it differently."

"It's not that long since I learned to ride myself," said Rennie in a quiet voice.

"I think you have to exercise some sort of authority," said Patrick. "I know that Sara and I used to observe each other and make suggestions, but that was different from actually teaching a class."

"At least we've got to know a few of the school ponies," commented Lettie, "I hope that will help with teaching the children."

"Linda said yesterday that we might take some of the other ponies out for a ride around the loch this afternoon," said Patrick, keen to continue exploring the countryside.

"I love the loch. It must be whish up here in the summer being able to swim and fish in it," said Janet.

"I'm looking forward to riding to the sea next week," said Charles. "There's not many beaches in Oxfordshire!"

"It's strange that a few of us live in Oxfordshire," commented Janet. "There's you, Charles and Susan. I live at the Thorneycrofts, although I'm originally from the north. Patrick, you live in Surrey, don't you? So, it's not that far to travel for us to have a get-together when we go home."

"Oh, yes! That would be fun," I commented, not able to resist the temptation to join in the conversation. "I'll ask Daddy if I can have a weekend party. We've plenty of rooms in our house and three bathrooms, and I can get some of my friends along to meet you."

"If I'm back down in Chatton, I hope I get invited too," butted in Jill.

"Of course. You'll be a celebrity," I said. It was hard to tell if Jill wanted to be the centre of attention or just one of the bunch, and not singled out.

"I can bring my friend, Ann Derry. She adores meeting new people, and you can all go in her address book."

"I remember her from your books," said Lettie shyly. "Is she going to marry that vet?"

"Well, it's not official yet, but it looks pretty likely," replied Jill. "We can invite him along too. He's a good egg."

"It must be every horse person's dream to marry a vet," said Janet.

"Or a farmer," added Rennie.

—

We finished breakfast, and all dashed over to the stables. I felt myself experiencing the needle, which was unusual for me. It was Noel who frequently suffered from this nervous condition. John had tacked up Skydiver, and I measured my stirrup leathers along my arm and put them down an extra hole as befitted a correct dressage position. John led the big grey gelding to the mounting block. He was more than a hand taller than Tranquil and much more solid. I mounted, and I was so high up that I could see Tranquil grazing in one of the cute little fields with stone walls.

I walked off to the indoor school, and the others rode over to the outside arena. Jill was taking the group this morning. She had taken a course at Porlock Vale to get qualified to be a riding instructor, so the plan was that she was going to pass on some of this knowledge.

I forgot my worries while in the saddle and experiencing Skydiver's long swinging stride. A lot of the things Major Holbrooke and Noel had been banging on about for years now made a lot more sense. That morning, I experienced those things first-hand, that had previously been merely notions, such as rhythm, cadence, and balance. This was the real thing. I even went so far as to wonder if I should ask Daddy to buy me a horse like this. But I loved Tranquil, and I didn't want to sell him. I had always wanted to keep my first pony, Beauty and let her have a foal, and then Daddy bought Golden Wonder off June Creswell. When I graduated to a horse, both ponies had been sold to the Lucien brothers, Nicholas and Jonathan. There were really only so many horses that one could own and then sell on. It was heartbreaking.

After an hour's expert instruction from the gorgeous Linda, the two judges, Mercedes and Mark, strutted over. I felt intimidated by both of them. They were impossibly glamorous and were the rising stars of the eventing world, always in *Horse and Hound*. I couldn't imagine that they would be impressed by my feeble efforts to ride an advanced dressage test.

Linda asked if I wanted her to prompt me, and I agreed with relief. I had been sure that after all my attempts at memorising the test, I had it down pat, but now I felt my mind dissipating under the stress of the occasion. However, it wasn't too bad once we got going and I remembered the aids for each of the pirouettes, and I had to say that Skydiver's extended trot across the arena really was like floating on air. I wished I could just go on and on, but then my test ended, and I saluted, remembered to smile at the judges, and left the arena on a loose rein giving Skydiver a grateful pat. I didn't suppose I'd get the highest marks or anything, but I had enjoyed myself hugely.

"How did your test go this morning?" asked Charles. "I was tempted to slip away to watch you, but Jill kept us hard at it, instilling the basics of how to be an instructor."

"It was fabulous fun," I replied. "Linda called out instructions, so I didn't get lost. Riding a proper dressage horse is a fab experience."

"Well, I'm tomorrow, and I'll be glad to get it over and done with. I've never even done a basic dressage test, and being thrown in the deep end with an advanced test is a bit much."

"You'll do brilliantly," I said to him kindly.

After lunch, we had a couple of hours to work on our jump-building projects that had to be finished by Monday afternoon. I absolutely adored jump building, and I was surprisingly creative when given an opportunity. Charles just went along with whatever I suggested. I had come up with three ideas which I sketched out. One was a jump with the wings shaped like butterfly wings and painted in beautiful gold, pink and pale blue colours. The other was a dragon with the head on one wing and the tail on the other. The third was meant to be a seascape with a mermaid on one side and a fish standing up on its tail with a trident on the other. Finally, we decided on the dragon, and Charles had suggested that we have flames coming out of its mouth.

We had to enlist the help of the part-time gardener who worked at the castle. He helped us cut out the wooden shapes with a tool called a jigsaw. It was like a little mechanical saw. The only way it made sense to me being called a jigsaw was that you might use it to make jigsaws. Then, I had drawn in the details with the dragon's beady eye, scales, claws on his feet and the brilliant orange, red and yellow flames coming out of his mouth. I loved this designing and painting. We had had to ask Mr Micheldever to get us some extra coloured paints when he drove into Kilkarny as the usual red, white, blue and greens were not enough for this ambitious project.

Charles was working on the flames using the paintbrush in a flourishing manner. I was carefully painting in the scales, which was rather tedious, but I was very pleased with the effect. Lettie and Rennie were on the other side of the workshop, totally engrossed with their painting. Lettie had sketched out two landscapes which they were using to decorate a wall. One of the scenes was nearly finished. It was a beautiful old-fashioned crooked house sitting on the edge of a wide river that moved slowly across the base of the wall. There were two incredibly realistic swans swimming on it. In the garden next to the cottage, she had painted a bay pony mare which was Martini, and the cutest little black pony.

Janet and Patrick had not been doing much with their jump, which was not at all original. Just an ordinary hogsback with some fill made up of wooden doors which they had decorated with a range of geometric shapes. As a jump, it was perfectly acceptable and probably much more interesting than usually found in the average showjumping competition. However, compared to our dragon and Lettie's scenery wall, it was rather dull.

Mrs Micheldever brought up afternoon tea on a tray and told us that the ponies were being saddled up for our ride and we were to set out in forty minutes. I would have liked to continue with our painting, but we had to stick to the schedule that was devised for us, and there were more than three days to finish my work of art.

"Here we have Prince," introduced John. "He's not a bad-looking chap but a slug of the first order. He will keep up with the others on a ride, but he'll just happily jog along at the back. Next is Turpin, a very ordinary looking creature, extremely quiet, used to be a cart horse but don't count that against him. He's a worthy animal and deserves respect."

"I think Charles and I should have these two," said Patrick. "As we're much the tallest of you all."

"Fair enough," said John. "Choose your mounts."

"I'll have Turpin," Patrick said, "as I think I'm all of an inch taller than Charles, and he can have Prince Slug."

"Here is another very reliable gentleman called Brownie, who is often ridden by Mr Micheldever or used as a pack animal during the shooting season. He's a kind old thing and surprisingly comfortable to ride in spite of his straight shoulders and short upright pasterns."

"I'll have him," said Janet. "A kind, quiet horse after Firestorm, will be an agreeable change."

"I think Lettie, as you are the shortest, you can have Oriole, a bundle of absolute ill-tempered stubbornness. Susan, you can have Rex, a Welsh pony who can beat any equine in a trotting race, and Rennie, you can have Misty. He was ridden in the bending race, but Star as the only other option at only 11 hh is definitely too small for you."

"In case you're thinking that you are too tall for such small ponies, can I remind you that the Mongolians, who are reputed to be some of the best horsemen in the world, all ride extremely small horses. I believe they stand in the stirrups and shoot bows and arrows or rifles," said Hugh in bracing tones.

"I think it's fun," I replied, trying to jolly everyone along.

We set off in a group, riding up the pathway between the small fields and arriving at the edge of the loch. The sun was shining, and dazzling light points danced on top of the wavelets.

"I don't mind riding these little ponies but let's hope we can take some of our horses on the ride to the sea," said Charles.

"It's good experience riding different horses," I told him placidly.

"Do you know what's on the agenda tomorrow afternoon?" asked Patrick.

"Hopefully we'll get to do a lot of work on our jumps," I replied.

"Well, I'm looking forward to being able to muck around on the cross-country course this weekend. Just have to get the teaching thing over and done with, then we can have some fun," said Charles.

"Trot on!" called John from the head of the group. "I thought I might take you up over this hill, there's a good view up here. Can't quite see the sea but a bit more scenery for you."

"Goodness, this is difficult to rise to the trot. I think I'll just stand in my stirrups," I said as Rex forged to the front. "Come on, Charles, keep up!" I called, laughing out loud with exhilaration, hanging on to Rex's thick mane to keep my balance.

We scrambled up a steep hill, the narrow rocky path winding to left and to right and back on itself.

"I can now see the advantage of these nippy little creatures," called Patrick. "I feel as if I'm on a trail climbing up into the Himalayas."

"Wouldn't it be fun to go trekking in the Himalayas?" I mused.

Charles looked at me in amazement.

"I had no idea you were so adventurous!" he exclaimed.

"Well, I don't think I really am. I was just imagining, daydreaming is one of my favourite subjects," I explained.

"I do want to visit Europe," he said quite seriously as if recommending himself to a difficult client. "I hadn't really thought of the wilder places like Asia, Africa and South America."

"No, no, you misunderstood," I tried to reassure him. "I'm just a homebody who likes to ride my horse, go to shows, and spend time with my friends."

He looked relieved at this. Perhaps, he thought he had got me entirely wrong.

"What is it like living with such wonderful views all the time?" Janet asked John. "They just fill the mind. Do you get used to it?"

"Not exactly used to it," said John. "I mean if it went away, I would certainly feel the loss."

70

"You can't live on a view. That's what Daddy says," I butted in.

"What does your father do for a crust?" asked Patrick politely.

"He's got a shoe factory," I replied, laughing. "That's not exactly exciting, but it is profitable. I mean, we all need shoes."

"I think it could be amazingly artistic," said Lettie behind me. "Think of the wonderful shoes that you could design. Shoes are really the ultimate accessory. That's what separates us from the animals. The ability to accessorise."

"How did you come up with that?" asked Patrick.

"It wasn't me. I read it in a magazine at the dentist, or somewhere like that," replied Lettie.

"Are you going to work in the factory?" asked Patrick.

I looked at him in astonishment. A vision of myself in a headscarf on the assembly line flashed before my eyes, with girls who were called Maud and Ada and Eunice. Of course, it had never occurred to me to go to work in the factory. Mummy and Valerie were very diminishing of the business. They never seemed to make the obvious link between it and our very comfortable lifestyle."

"I hadn't thought," I said slowly.

"With your artistic streak, think of the shoes you could design," said Lettie dreamily.

This was a revelation. So obvious, but it had never occurred to me before. My future had lain before me as nothing but a troublesome conundrum. I wasn't like Noel and Henry. Henry had already embarked on his military career and Noel was going to scale the glorious heights of equestrian achievement. I was planning to marry a young man who was still a mere schoolboy. I was going to have to fill in the years until we both grew up. I could work in the factory. If nothing else, it would make my father happy, and he deserved to be happy. He worked so hard and put up with so much. I had found the answer to my life on a hillside in the Scottish Highlands.

We rode back to the stables, and my head was full of visions. I wanted to sit down immediately and start sketching shoes, elegant high heels with silver buckles and tiny intricate straps. Square toes, round toes and pointed toes. I needed to consult some of those fashion magazines that my mother and Valerie were always poring over. Then it struck me. Boots! Boots were the things. I wore them all the time and never gave them a second thought. What utterly delicious things you could do with boots!

"You're looking a bit dazed," said Charles with concern.

71

"I've just had the most brilliant thought. I can design shoes and work in the factory with Daddy while you're going to Oxford until we get married," I replied happily. Then I clapped my hand over my mouth. I was such a klutz. I had broken the cardinal rule, never presume upon a man proposing. I looked at Charles in dismay, thinking that after this remark, he would never want to talk to such a presumptuous girl as me again.

He laughed.

"Yes, you can," he cried. "And perhaps I can work in the factory as well and take it over, and we'll live happily ever after."

He held out his hand, and I took it. There was a lovely warm buzz of electricity running between us. The future was settled. It was only a matter of deciding how many children we would have, and they would be the next generation of West Barsetshire Pony Club members.

On Friday morning, it was more practising instructing. I had been instructed endlessly over the years, so it was just a matter of remembering what the Major, or Henry, or Noel would say to the other riders. Fortuitously, Mrs Micheldever turned up with mugs of coffee on a tray, and I was able to skip over to the indoor school and watch Charles do his dressage test.

I must admit I had wondered how he might manage with his leg. I won't say that you didn't notice it, especially when he had his stirrups longer at the optimum dressage length. He did make sure to sit squarely in the saddle, so his weight wasn't on one side more than the other, thus unbalancing the horse. It almost seemed as if Skydiver was aware of Charles' having one weaker leg, and he did his best to compensate for his rider's shortcomings. They did a creditable test, and I felt myself glowing with pride that this brave young man who worked so hard to overcome his physical disabilities had chosen to love and adore me.

Last night we had gone outside to be alone, and he had held my hand tenderly, and we had kissed in the rose garden. It had been one of the most thrilling experiences of my life in one way, but in another, it felt entirely natural, as if it was just was just entirely the way it should be.

PART SIX
by Patrick Huntingdon

Chapter Eleven

On Wednesday morning, it was my turn to do a dressage test on Skydiver. I had watched Janet do hers the day before, and I knew she was miles better than me. This hadn't detracted from the experience, which I had enjoyed immensely. I was used to riding a larger horse from my experience on Scarlet Pimpernel, and I had more or less learned everything I knew on the lively Adonis, but Skydiver was something else. He walked forward with a long, lively stride, and I could literally feel his hindlegs come beneath him, providing impulsion, which had the related effect of raising his head but bending at the poll. He did not arch his neck in a vain attempt to escape the action of the bit, which many people mistakenly thought was collection. We floated through the test, and I felt like I was riding in one of the Spanish Riding School performances. I wished that Sara, my younger sister, could have been here to see it and to try him. She would have enjoyed it so much.

I was standing first in the competition, but the current score was only for the bending and the points of the horse. There was still the dressage test. Undoubtedly, I would be way down in the ranking, and my fence construction with Janet would probably mean we came last. I had absolutely no hope of winning the final prize of a weekend in Vienna. Although I had daydreamed of sweeping Valerie off her feet with such a tremendous holiday, Sara would never forgive me if I didn't take her.

I know that brothers and sisters often engage in a fight to the death during their childhood, but Sara and I are very close. For years we were locked together in a hopeless mutual passion for horses and all things horsey. This battle went on for years as we engaged in a fantasy world where Sara rode a fidgety chestnut mare called Firefly, and I had a fiery black stallion called Demon. Of course, children are not usually mounted on stallions, but this made no difference to us as we cavorted down Bond Street on our imaginary steeds who never walked a step and were constantly dancing, prancing, rearing or bucking and bolting.

We lived in one of the outer suburbs of London, and finally, our parents agreed that we should have outfits and two dozen riding lessons each for Christmas. The most superior of the three riding schools in our area was selected. I must point out that our family was not poor or struggling financially. On the contrary, we were very well off. It was just that although Mummy and Daddy were perfectly good and reasonable in every way, they were Unhorsey, with a capital U. We didn't know from whence this aversion sprung, but it was a Great Truth.

We went to Captain Stefinski's establishment, rode Copper and Silver in the covered yard, and hacked across Marston Common and into Sackville Park on Jonathon and Treasure. Our parents had planned that this would put paid to our equestrian ambitions forever, but to their horror Captain Stefinski told them we were promising riders. So they decided the answer was to push us into tennis, and we were given swanky outfits and coaching. We were even taken to Wimbledon and had seats to watch the action on Centre Court.

We kept on hoping that our parents would relent and we would be allowed to return to Captain Stefinski's, but after the tennis stint, I was sent off to do squash, and Sara had dancing lessons. Then there was skating. Our parents were determined that we should be 'all-rounders'. We were carted off to a series of London museums and pantomimes. Then I was pushed into cricket, and Sara had to take up eurhythmics.

There was one interlude when Sara's friend, Robina, had a pony called Seagull, and we had a chance to ride it, but our parents weren't keen.

Then a miracle occurred. Sara and I went with our mother to stay with the Merrimans, who lived in the country near East

Minster. We were there for the whole of the summer holidays while our father had to go overseas on a business trip. The Merrimans had horses, and we could ride, which was just the beginning. We befriended the most adorable pony called Adonis, who was an Anglo-Arab that had been purchased for one of the Merriman children, Jane, but they didn't get on, and after a few disasters, he was written off as a rogue and unrideable. Secretly, Sara and I rode him. Then it all came out, and to cut a long story short, the Merrimans declared that they were giving him to us. Mummy and Daddy arranged that he was to stay at Captain Stefinski's as they didn't want a loose box in the garden.

Our parents had now accepted that we were indubitably horsey, and nothing would change that. Then I shot up like a beanpole. By the following year, I was far too tall to ride Adonis, who was 14.2 hh. Fortunately, there were quite a few other horses on livery at the riding stables, and I became friends with Valerie, who was my own age.

She was a terrific girl, as tall as me, with long, straight brown hair and very kind and intelligent brown eyes. She has a lovely horse called Scarlet Pimpernel but not much time to ride as she is studying like mad to do well in her exams so she can study medicine. So she told me that I was doing her a favour by riding Scarlet Pimpernel. He was very obliging, well-mannered and not a bad jumper.

When I won the competition in *Riding*, it was a huge shock. I had not wanted to enter, but I was carried along on the wave of Sara's enthusiasm that had me jot down a few thoughts on why it was I loved riding. I must admit that Sara gave me the main ideas that I used in my entry, and it seemed grossly unfair that it was me that won the fortnight in Scotland. Really, it should have been her. Valerie was more than happy that I should take Scarlet Pimpernel, and here I was.

I think I must have been the least experienced rider of the prize winners, having wasted so much of my youth being forced to

engage in other types of sporting activities. Sara and I had often dreamed of huge success in showjumping or the show ring, but the reality was that we would never be more than enthusiastic amateurs. We were not going to become professional horsemen or horsewomen. We would not work in the equine world of business. I was probably going to study law, and Sara, who might possibly have qualified as a riding instructor, had been discovered as a very good linguist and was studying French and German at an advanced level at school and was being encouraged to continue her studies overseas. She was somewhat nonplussed by this skill which she was exhibiting, but we talked about the possibilities of studying dressage in Germany, and she went along with our parents and teachers hoping that it might all work out.

It was Charles' turn to ride Skydiver and do his dressage test on Friday morning. The rest of us were to practise instructing in the outdoor arena. Linda and Jill arranged for us so that four of us were riding school students, and the instructor had to take us through the lesson that they had planned. We had each been allocated a class classified as good riders, who could canter and jump with some proficiency, medium riders who could canter and jump a bit, advanced beginners who were able to canter but more by good luck than skill, and beginner beginners who were still mastering the rising trot and maintaining some semblance of a correct riding position. Janet was to take the most advanced of the students, who were considered the cream of the crop of the riding school. She had decided to go through more advanced movements such as turning on the forehand, transitioning from walk to canter with the correct aids, and then a go at shoulder-in. Susan and Charles were each given a medium rider class and worked together on a lesson plan. Charles had never instructed in his life, and this joint venture was meant to help him to get the hang of it. Lettie and I were each given a class of advanced beginners, and Rennie was given the beginner beginners.

There was a lot of raucous tomfoolery when the prize winners had to practise being advanced beginners and beginner beginners, with people hanging off their saddles, sitting backwards, tipping onto their horses' necks and generally behaving in a way that was most unlike any beginner I had ever known.

"You're not taking this seriously," remonstrated Linda, probably thinking she might lose all her riding school students by letting us loose on them.

"We'll behave at the weekend," said Susan trying to reassure her, "we'll be models of propriety."

Linda raised her eyebrows in an expression of disbelief.

I had spent ages devising a lesson based on my memory of our first lessons at Captain Stefinski's. That now seemed like something from the distant past. Life had moved on tremendously since Sara and I had gone for our first lessons.

We were given the good news that we had a free afternoon at lunch. So we could work on our jump construction, have a go at the cross-country course, ride around the loch or lie under a tree in the garden. Everyone looked relieved at this. There is just so much organised activity that an ordinary person can take. I imagined what it must be like in the army, being constantly scheduled into events. Certainly not for me!

I was tossing up between reading a book in the garden or taking Scarlet Pimpernel for a walk around the loch when Mark Lansdowne tapped me on the shoulder and asked me if he could have a private word. I felt very nervous. Mark was not exactly approachable, and we always got the idea that he would rather be doing anything but being a judge in this competition. I had no idea why he was singling me out, and I felt uneasy. I followed him out of the dining room into the passageway.

"I wanted you to come with me this afternoon, ride one of my horses for me. I want to do some jumping around the cross-country, give them some training," he barked at me like a sergeant-major.

"Yes, of course," I found myself saying, quailing in the face of his commanding demeanour.

"Let's go down to the stables now," he said.

Whereas the prize winners had their mounts tacked up by John and Hugh, this was not the case with Mark.

"I'm riding Twillen, and this lad is riding Archer," he said to John when we walked into the yard. John looked at him blankly and turned away without a word. This did make me wonder. John was always cheerful and obliging whenever any of our prize winners needed help.

Mark looked thunderous but didn't push the point. I knew Mark had some of his competition horses here at Blainstock, but I had no idea how this arrangement worked. Now, it became apparent that he had to attend to his own horses when he wanted to ride. This piqued my curiosity. He suggested we ride once around the loch and then go onto the cross-country course.

We walked up through the small fields until we came to the loch. I watched Mark riding Twillen, a rather plain brown horse, 16.3 hh, a thoroughbred gelding. He walked out with a lively, measured step and seemed well-schooled. Although unprepossessing in appearance, he might well be fantastic at dressage and jumping. Mark certainly rode well. His seat in the saddle was firm, and I imagined that it would take a lot to dislodge him.

I couldn't resist questioning Mark about why he kept his horses in Scotland when he lived down south.

"Tell me," I asked in a voice that quivered with nervous bravado. "Why are some of your competition horses here when you are based in Oxfordshire?"

For a minute, he looked furious. He stared at me, probably thinking that I was an impertinent nobody. I waited for a blast of fury. Then he relented.

"All my horses were here at Blainstock until last year," he replied. "The facilities were all built specifically for me by my Uncle Richard years ago. Then he married Catherine, and Jill Crewe turned up. Then the family trust was stolen, and now Blainstock Stables is run as a business by Jill and three of her mates, and I'm pushed out."

"Gosh!" I said, truly shocked. "That is rather hard luck, you being family and all."

"Yes," he replied. "I did a deal with them. They got Firestorm and Shadow, and in return, I got full livery for my horses."

"Oh, I see," I said slowly. "That's why they don't saddle up for you and things like that. Do they ride the horses for you while you're away?"

"Yes, exercising the horses is part of the deal. They get ridden four times a week. The rest of the time, they get turned out in the fields. They're not schooled or jumped or anything like that," he replied. "That's why I need to ride them now. See how they're getting on, and give them some jumping practice. After that, I have to make some decisions about what to do with them."

I wondered why he had chosen to confide in me, but I guess I was there and asked the question.

"What have you done with them up until now?" I asked, veering away from the awkward story of tangled, unhappy family relationships.

"Archer, who you're riding, I've had him for three years. He's ten, and if he doesn't do some serious competing, he will be too old. I bought him off a young woman who had him as a hunter, but he was too strong for her. He's a good jumper, but he needs more dressage training, and that's not my thing. Dressage is what you have to do to get on with the cross-country and the showjumping."

I looked at Mark, finding a new respect for him. He seemed ready to admit his weaknesses. Although it could be argued that dressage was the basis of any discipline, it wasn't my place to say that to him.

"He's a good-looking horse," I said. He was at least 16 hh, probably 16.2 hh, strongly built. Perhaps his neck was not long enough, his shoulder a trifle straight, but he certainly had an impressive set of hindquarters.

"He lacks speed around the cross-country, so he has to be in tip-top condition to be able to gallop around in good time," said Mark.

"It seems a shame that Linda can't do some flat work with him. On the other hand, she is pretty good at dressage," I ventured, thinking that this was probably shaky ground.

We walked forward. This horse was no Skydiver, but nor was he like Scarlet Pimpernel. He was solid as a brick wall. Whereas Skydiver was elegant, and Scarlet Pimpernel was flexible and springy, this horse felt like an oversize cob. He was workmanlike. His spirit seemed very calm and deliberate, and I suspected he would be obedient, like a well-trained soldier who followed the chain of command.

"Trot on," said Mark.

Twillen and Archer kept in step together.

"They're stable mates," explained Mark, as if he were reading my thoughts.

"Now canter," barked Mark as the path became wide and sandy.

I sat down and gave the correct aids to canter. Archer responded willingly. He might not have mastered the finer points of dressage, but his basic schooling seemed sound. After we had gone around the loch, we headed to the cross-country course.

Chapter Twelve

Mark leaned down and opened the gate, and we rode into the field where the cross-country course was set up. From this vantage point, you could see most of the jumps. It was spread out before us like a figure eight.

"I designed this course myself, you know," said Mark, with a tangible note of bitterness in his voice. "There are 35 jumps, and a lot of them are based on jumps from Burghley and Badminton. So I'll take the lead. You follow, several lengths behind."

I was excited and nervous all at once. Determined to ride to the very best of my ability, I wanted to prove to Mark that he had not made a mistake in asking me to ride with him. The first jump was, as is the case with all first jumps, inviting and easy, an unassuming log pile. Next was a series of post-and-rails with a ditch in front of them. Mark headed straight for the highest of them. I quailed a little as it was a substantial four-feet high, but I didn't think Mark would approve if I diverted to the next lowest. Archer sailed over without hesitation.

I was daunted at the sight of the Vicarage Vee, a famous jump at Burghley. Mark didn't pause and headed straight for the middle, neither the narrowest V-end nor the widest. I resisted the temptation to shut my eyes and let Archer carry me over. I might never have an opportunity like this again. Instead, I was determined to relish every moment.

Next, there was a steep bank, and I sat well back, so I didn't tip forward and end up on his neck. Archer slid down on his strong, solid haunches, and I really did feel safe as houses. After that, I settled into the rhythm. I felt the flow of the course. With the competent leadership of Mark and Twillen, who must have jumped this course a hundred times, we flew around over all the jumps, including a row of barrels, a huge garden seat, a very narrow stile, a tree trunk that was raised above ground level, and a square jump where we jumped through the middle. Then we galloped through the designated finish. I was breathless but filled with elation. I had never experienced anything like this before.

If I had hoped for effusive congratulations from Mark, then I would have been kidding myself. I marvelled at the way that Archer had jumped. He was so experienced. I could feel him picking his take-off point. He also jumped economically, with no huge unnecessary leaps. He was a perfect judge of height and width, and I thought how much a horse like this could teach a rider.

We trotted, then walked to warm down the horses. Mark asked, "Where do you live?" His attitude was intent. There was purpose behind this enquiry, no mere social platitude.

"In Surrey, outside of London. My sister and I have a pony, but he's only 14.2 hh, and I've outgrown him. I brought up a horse of a friend of mine. I ride him quite a bit. He's kept at Captain Stefinski's riding school," I replied. As well-known as Captain Stefinski's stable is in our home town, it was unlikely that Mark would ever have heard of him. I felt like I was in a job interview, and this intuition turned out to be correct.

"Would you like to lease Archer for six months?" asked Mark.

"Gosh, do you think I'm good enough?" I asked in surprise.

"You ride pretty well. He's not hard to manage if you have an ounce of gumption, and it would be good if you could do some flat work with him. I don't mind if you jump him," replied Mark, magnanimously as if he was doing me a tremendous favour. Only later, when I had time to consider this, I realised how advantageous such an arrangement was for Mark. It meant I would bear all the expense, do the flat work, and get the horse fit, ready for Mark to jump on and compete in the autumn three-day events when the six months were up. And Archer would already be located in the south of England when the time came rather than in the depths of Scotland. But, when he offered, I was swept away with the idea of having such a horse to ride and that Mark seemed to think that I was up to it.

"I would have to get my parents to agree," I replied, thinking I must sound like a kid.

We rode on in silence. My mind was racing.

"If I am leasing him, that means I might enter him in competitions?" I asked.

Mark looked thoughtful.

"Yes, why not. You're ambitious. I like that."

I thought about it. Six months was a pretty short lease. I might just get to the point where we were ready to compete, and Mark would swan in and take him back. But, on the other hand, I could showjump him all summer.

"What has he done in the past?" I asked. "What competitions?"

"We did about a dozen one-day events. He was good, clear in the cross-country and showjumping but always low down in the dressage. He doesn't have free movement, certainly no expressiveness, as they call it."

"Did you three-day event him at all?"

"Yes, we entered a few. Again, he went clear in the jumping in the novice events, but his dressage marks were always at the bottom of the field."

"Do you really think I could improve his dressage? I'm pretty well a novice myself," I replied, kicking myself for my hesitancy and for not grabbing this opportunity and running with it.

"Whatever you do in terms of improving him is better than him up here treading water being ridden around the loch by John or Hugh four times a week. Plus, he needs to get fit. You could at least do that."

I thought about this for a while. From my own point of view, I was being offered a horse of high quality that I could never afford to buy, and I was pretty certain no one else would offer to lease me a horse like this!

We got back to the stables, and without waiting for the staff to help, I unsaddled Archer and led him into his box. I spent a long time rubbing him down and trying to get a feel for him. He was such a matter-of-fact horse, not soppy nor sentimental. I looked out into the stable yard, and Mark had walked away. I didn't fool myself that Mark might suddenly want to be chums with me. He saw me as useful. I didn't mind. I was buzzing with the possibility of taking Archer to Captain Stefinski's. I was sure that Valerie would be mightily impressed to see me mounted on such a horse, and it meant that we could ride together.

After I had helped to do the evening feeds and water, I went back to the castle. I ran into Mrs Micheldever in the hall.

"I was wondering if I might make a phone call to my parents?"

"Oh, Patrick! Is something wrong?" she asked.

"No, no, not at all." I could have blurted out what had happened, but instinctively I felt that the arrangement proposed by Mark was confidential.

She suggested that I go into the office where I would have some privacy.

"Hello," said my mother on the other end of the line.

"It's Patrick," I blurted out.

"Is something wrong?" she asked.

"No, not at all. Everything up here is going well. I don't think I will win the weekend to go to Vienna, but it's fun. A really decent set of people."

"Poor Sara missed out, didn't she?"

"The thing is," I said, cutting straight to the point, "I've been offered this stupendous horse for lease for six months. He belongs to Mark Lansdowne, who is a well-known three-day eventer."

"Really!" she exclaimed. "You must have impressed him with your riding skills."

"It would mean we would have to pay the costs of keeping him at Captain Stefinski's," I went on. "Do you think we could afford another horse?"

"But what about being away at school? Would it be worth it?" she asked.

"There's only the next term, and Sara could exercise him and I could ride him a lot through the summer," I replied. "I could take him to some of the shows and do some showjumping, and then in the autumn he'd go back to Mark, when I'm really going to have to knuckle down and study for my exams."

"Yes, I can see the logic of that," replied my mother. "I'll have to talk to your father. When do we have to decide by?"

"I suppose before I leave here, then he can come down in the box with Scarlet Pimpernel. If you agree, we must ensure that Captain Stefinski can have him."

"Don't worry, darling. I'm sure we can arrange it all. I think we need to make up for the fact that it took us so long to realise just how much this horse riding means to you and Sara," said my mother. I was shocked. It was the first time that she had acknowledged all those years when they had stood in the way of our horse dreams.

That night at dinner, I sat there like a dummy. My mind was filled with visions of riding Archer. I began to think about his dressage training. I would like to ask Linda to help me with some ideas for what type of work needed to be done, but it was awkward. I had become aware of the rivers of ill-feeling that were running beneath the Blainstock Stables. It was not the Highland paradise that it seemed. Human nature always triumphed over the Utopian ideal. I did think that I might seek the advice of Janet. Not only was she very pleasant and helpful, but she was also talented, a true professional.

I was fairly certain that my parents were alright with it, but I had to have their definite agreement. I didn't want to pressure them, but I had to know one way or the other. I thought perhaps if I told Mark that I would take him, then perhaps Mercedes might be able to give me some pointers.

After dinner, I sloped off to the library, found a tome on dressage written by Henry Wynmalen and took it up to my bedroom. I had a notepad and pencil, and I began to make notes. It was difficult. It wasn't that Archer had behavioural problems. If anything, he was punctilious in his correctness.

How did one develop a sense of flair and fluid movement and bring a horse on from what seemed like soldierly discipline that left no room for 'expressiveness'.

The next morning there was 0a buzz around the breakfast table. We were scheduled to conduct our riding lessons, and everyone was discussing their different instructors over the years and the various methods that one practised to improve one's riding.

"I wish Noel and Henry were here," sighed Susan, "they've taught as many lessons as I've had hot dinners."

"Just channel Noel," I said, perhaps a little sharply. I hadn't slept much last night, and I'd heard so much about the blessed West Barsetshire Pony Club that it was like a broken record.

Charles glared at me. He obviously thought that I was being hard on Susan, who he believed could do no wrong. Rennie was talking earnestly to Janet, asking for her advice on how to tackle her class. Bevan was in a deep discussion with Mr Micheldever,

asking him about classes of sailing boats. I couldn't follow the differentiation between a gaff-rigged, sloop, schooner, or Bermuda.

We were on our last cup of coffee before trooping over to the riding school when Mercedes and Mark walked in. I smiled hesitantly at Mark, and he nodded at me. This was more attention than he bestowed on any of the other prize winners. I saw Jill flash a quick look at us. She was certainly hyper-alert when it came to Mark. I wondered whether she thought he might favour me in marking the competitions.

Linda, Hugh and John hadn't joined us for breakfast. They would be preparing the riding school ponies for the morning classes. Janet was first, teaching the advanced class scheduled for nine o'clock.

The rest of us sat on a bench on the side of the arena and watched with interest. Bridie McIver, one of the children from the village general store, was riding their family's leased pony, Tippy. There were four McIver children, and they shared one pony between them. Tippy was very pretty, finely built, with a dished face and huge soul-wrenching eyes. Although at 16 years old, she was slowing down a bit. Bridie was a very keen rider and had been coming on by leaps and bounds.

Cassie Frayne was that child who was spoilt rotten by her mother and considered herself a cut above the other children. She had perfectly curled blonde hair, china-blue eyes, and a pouting rosebud mouth. Matching her prissy looks, she had an air of superiority and a very irritating smugness. Her mother had promised to buy her a show pony, but so far, they had not found the one that suited them, so today, Cassie was mounted on Cammie, the best-looking riding school ponies. Usually, Cammie was considered the best pony on offer, but today Ellie had been mounted on Black Boy, Jill's old pony. He had just arrived at the stables, and Mrs Frayne buttonholed Linda and was cross-examining her why Cassie had not been given the new mount.

I did admire Linda for her tact and restraint.

"Black Boy is the old pony of Jill Crewe," she explained. "He is more of a beginner's pony."

"Oh, I see," said Mrs Frayne.

"Can I introduce you to some of the prize winners who are with this us for a fortnight? You know they've won a competition in the magazine *Riding*," said Linda, cleverly distracting this annoying mother. "Susan Barington-Brown, and Charles Ravenscroft." She shot a meaningful look at Susan behind Mrs Frayne's back. Susan began chatting away, asking about Cassie and agreeing that she was a splendid rider. Charles stood there nodding, a little out of his social depth but admiring Susan's artful line in meaningless patter.

Linda called the riding school students to line up and introduced Janet, who was their instructor. Mark and Mercedes were standing at the ready with their clipboards and pencils to make notes. There were only five students in the class, one other girl on Copperplate and another on Bonnie. I admired the way Janet took them through their paces. She had them all successfully transitioning from walk to canter without a misstep of trot and then explained the complicated aids of shoulder-in, which they all achieved to some degree or another.

My mind wandered back to Archer. I was planning to ring home again tonight to see if my parents had agreed to me having him. I was hoping that I would be able to start work on him up here, getting some much-needed direction before he came down south with me.

PART SEVEN
by Rennie Jordan

Chapter Thirteen

I was the odd one out of the prize winners. But being the odd one out is not unusual for me. I'm used to it. I'm sure they all thought I was just a kid, about the same age as Lettie Lonsdale. However, I'm actually eighteen years old, as old as Janet Fawley. I kept this under my hat. It was somehow easier to be treated kindly - as just a kid. I certainly wasn't a serious contender for the grand prize. Of course, I would love to go to Vienna and watch the Spanish Riding School, but just this trip to the Scottish Highlands was exciting enough for me. Probably too exciting as I was getting more and more nervous about not only the dressage test but much worse than that, instructing at the riding school and being watched and judged.

As you can tell, I am a timid character. This is mainly because I suffered not one, but two horrendous and calamitous events as a child. First, when I was a tot, I was in a house that exploded and conscious for the entire time that I was buried. Then five years ago, I was in a car crash and saw my mother killed.

My Aunt Lucy came to look after my younger brother, Robin, and me. She thought that I was too passive. That I merely submitted to my psychological condition. My mind tricked me, and I found that on occasions, my hands just stopped working, and my knees grew weak and would not support my body.

Everything came to a head when I was sneaking a ride on an unbroken colt called Templar and fell off and broke my arm and collar bone and cracked two ribs. I had done this because I knew that the only thing I wanted to do in the world was with horses, and I had been desperate. It had all come right in a most wonderful way, and I went to stay at Miss Brandon's riding school at Kingwood. My father paid a small amount for my keep, and I received free riding lessons in exchange for me working with the horses. It was a dream come true.

I suppose it was my strange psychological condition that had caught the attention of the judges of the *Riding* competition. Perhaps I was the token 'good work', although Charles Ravenscroft had a wonky leg from polio. Still, he wasn't particularly in need of charity as he had his own showjumper and had even won a Foxhunter competition in his first season showjumping.

My life hadn't stopped when I went to Miss Brandon's riding stable. I was seventeen years old then and looked much younger. For some bizarre reason, a man called Maurice fell in love with me. I was not interested and ended up running away to work for a dealing stable which was guilty of all sorts of bad practices, drugging vicious horses to sell them is the worst of it.

This had resulted in the death of a young boy, and I could not bear to stay there any longer. I had gone home and found that my father was going to marry the delightful Miss Brandon, and Maurice's affections had switched back to Sally, and they were getting married. I even had an understanding with a boy my age, Morgan, that we might marry and go to Wales and have a farm.

Now all this was what one could call a very satisfactory happy ending, but life isn't like that. You can't neatly tie up your life like a parcel upon age eighteen. As far as my riding went, I was still lacking experience. I had never jumped, hunted or done any instruction so this fortnight at Blainstock Castle was a huge challenge. The others were certainly kind to me and tried to include me, but I wasn't in their league. They were all much more experienced riders and had owned their own ponies and horses for years, except Janet. They talked about competitions they had entered, their prospects in the future, and their equestrian careers, and I listened carefully, drinking in every detail. I didn't envy them their grand dreams and ambitious plans. After all the trauma in my life, I was more than content to live safely in the bosom of my family and look forward to a comfortable married life with Morgan.

I think that winning the points of the horse competition didn't do me much good. I felt like I was under a very uncomfortable harshly illuminating spotlight. Then there was the reported wailing in the night. It had been me having a nightmare. Now, I was terrified that I would fall to my knees, not be able to get up, and everyone would know what was wrong with me. It was the instruction thing that was preying on my mind.

Linda and Jill were helping us to prepare for this ordeal. We even had to write out a lesson plan that had never occurred to me before. The best I could think of was making the students walk in a circle and sayings things like, 'heels down', 'hands still', and 'look between the pony's ears.'

We sat down to Friday lunch, and they were all asking Charles about his dressage test that morning.

"How did it feel?" asked Susan.

"Amazing," he replied. "You know, I thought that jumping was the best thing in the world, but this dressage lark certainly has its merits."

"You sound like you've been converted," said Lettie with a sly grin. "You know dressage is just training. That's what it means in French, "*dresser*" is the verb 'to train'."

"I know that's the theory. But riding a horse like Skydiver in an advanced test is like dancing on the stage at a theatre," argued Charles, who was clearly in a 'topped up' state of mind.

I was scheduled to teach my beginners' class on Saturday, and I woke up clammy at midnight on Friday night. My mouth was dry, and I feared that I had been screaming. I lay in the dark, barely breathing, seeing if I had disturbed anyone who might be padding up and down the corridor listening out for more wails and gnashing of teeth. I must admit I was thinking of packing up and jumping on a train to go back home. I knew I didn't belong with this crowd, and as interesting as it was, I didn't think I would be able to cope.

On Saturday morning, Janet was teaching first, and I sat by myself watching her. She was so self-assured and competent. I knew that I was never going to be like that. I had my lesson plan notes on my lap and reviewed them again. It wasn't that long since Miss Brandon had been teaching me this same sort of stuff. All I had to do was put myself in the centre of the arena and pretend I was her and that the students were me.

Linda suggested that I might like to go along to the stable yard as the ponies for my class would be there, and I could assist the riders in mounting and adjusting their stirrup leathers. In addition, it would help me to remember their names and I could chat with them a little. It was a good idea and held back the growing tide of nervousness that was invading my body. I knew that it was ridiculous to get so worked up about delivering a one-hour lesson to a group of young beginners, but nothing I told myself helped dissipate my fear of chewing at my intestines like a nest of rats.

John and Hugh were saddling the ponies, and the first of the riders was there – a very small boy. I introduced myself.

"I'm Rennie, and I am taking the class this morning," I told him.

"Tommy," he announced and thrust out a small hand, which I shook.

"Which pony are you riding?" I asked.

"I have been riding Tommy, but today I'm upgrading," he confided proudly. "I'm on Rex."

"Oh yes, I know him. He's the best trotting pony in the world," I replied. Susan had been riding him when we went up around the loch.

"I'm very good at rising to the trot," declared Tommy.

"Good on you," I said.

Two girls had just been dropped in the yard. I made my way over to introduce myself.

"I'm Rennie," I said to them, "I'm taking your lesson today."

"Sheila," replied a very bright-eyed young girl. "We know all about it. You're one of the prize winners who have come up here from down south."

"That's right," I affirmed.

"I ride Taffy," she stated with a distinct proprietorial note in her high-pitched voice. "He is rather cranky, but I think we have come to an understanding."

"I love that dun colour," I volunteered, looking at the ill-tempered little monster with his mean eyes and swishing tail.

"Audrey," said Sheila, referring to the quiet mouse-like girl with large round glasses that gave her a distinctively owlish appearance, "she rides Prince. He looks after her."

"Yes, he is a lovely quiet fellow," I said.

"I thought we might do some gymkhana games after we've done some riding practice," I said. "What are your favourites?"

"Well, trotting races mean I win every time," declared Sheila, "but we had great fun when we did a sort of a version of it riding pillion, mixed in with a walk, trot and canter relay. I was up behind Cassie on Taffy, and we came second."

"I'm not sure we've got enough riders for that," I said. "But I don't see why we couldn't double up and ride around two on a pony. That might be fun." So much for the carefully laid plans of my prepared lesson.

Bobby, my fourth student, was late, and John told us to go ahead and start, and he would bring Bobby over when he arrived.

I was flustered at this blip in the arrangements. I took some deep breaths and told myself I had to think flexibly and just roll with the punches. Mercedes and Mark were watching attentively from the side lines. I was very conscious that my voice was high-pitched and breathless. I was terrified that my knees would go beneath me, and I would lie helpless on the ground in front of everyone. It had happened before and was worse than those dreams when you are naked in front of a fully-clothed crowd.

Somehow, I muddled my way through the lesson. Linda had put in some ideas for extra things so I had a range of options if one didn't seem to be working out. I got them all to walk around, picked on just one position fault of each rider, and encouraged them to improve. Tommy had a habit of waving his arms and legs around as windmills. He might have gotten away with this when he was riding the leading rein pony Star, but Rex was a different kettle of fish. Sheila's hands were too high, Audrey always looked down, and Bobby thrust his feet out in front of him.

I asked them all to trot, and things got rather disorganised. Tommy could indeed rise to the trot, but he went up so high that by the time he'd come down to the saddle, he'd missed a beat. Sheila was probably the best of the bunch, but Taffy, in his mean-spirited way, had to be constantly niggled to keep going. Audrey was tipping far too far forward, which didn't help to keep the lazy bones, Prince, from moving any faster than a disreputable shamble. Bobby was riding Oriole, another bad-tempered pony, who swished his tail and laid his ears back at any other pony that came within two strides of him.

The games I had thought up seemed to help. The children became more enthusiastic and competitive, which helped them push the ponies a little beyond their riding school stupor. I suggested we practise the pillion thing, thinking that collaborative effort was good for the character. This was a little ironic, seeing that I was such a loner myself.

I put Tommy up behind the cautious Audrey and Sheila behind Bobby, and they walked the length of the arena and turned and trotted. I hoped that none of them would fall off - in retrospect,

it was a risky manoeuvre. Having a student fall off and injure themselves would have to send me to the bottom of the competition.

Finally, my watch showed me that we had passed fifty minutes, and I called them all in and gave them a quick talk. I remembered to say something good about each of them and reminded them of the main thing I had focused on with their riding positions.

I staggered over to the seat where the other prize winners were sitting.

"Oh, well done!" said Susan, who seemed to have boundless kindness and positivity. I couldn't imagine being someone so happy and pleased with the world, but she certainly had a cheering-up effect on those around her. I could imagine her saying to herself last thing at night, 'isn't it lovely to be lovely me.' You could cure a migraine just by leaning on her shoulder. She exuded an air of such health and well-being. No wonder Charles had fallen deeply in love with her.

There was one more lesson before lunch: Charles with a group of more advanced beginners. I decided that he didn't need me watching to give him moral support, and I slid out the door and made my way back to the castle to spend some time on my own, to recover from the morning's trauma.

I went up to my room and threw myself on the bed. I was shaking, a strange nervous reaction that I sometimes had to stress. I began to rock gently back and forth and finally fell asleep. A tapping on my door woke me. It was Jill, who had come up to find me as lunch was started. I had felt rather intimidated when it came to Jill. She was one of those jolly people who were so full to the brim with self-confidence that she seemed to exist on a different planet.

"Are you alright, Rennie?" she asked.

"Yes, yes," I declared, jumping up. But then, I had to sit on the edge of the bed as dizziness hit me.

"There's no hurry. You look a bit peaky. Thought you might not want to miss lunch, but I can bring you something up if you like."

"No, no," I said, hating the idea that I should be treated like a special case. "I'll come down, just give me a minute."

"How do you think we're doing? You know with the way we've arranged things?" she asked.

"I think it's fantastic here," I said sincerely. "You have an amazing setup. Copperplate, she's an absolute darling, better than any other riding school horse I've ever ridden."

"She wasn't meant to be a riding school horse. She was my second horse, but with the way things have turned out, she's gone into the riding school."

"Black Boy, he was your pony too," I said, trying to think of something to say.

"Yes, that's right. He got sold, but I tracked him down and got him back. I'll never let him go again."

I was surprised that she was so sentimental about her pony, and she shot up in my estimation. We went down to lunch together.

Chapter Fourteen

Susan was teaching her riding lesson after lunch. Lettie and Patrick would have their turn on Sunday morning. There were five of us planning to jump around the cross-country that afternoon, and Jill was also coming with us. It would be good to get out and ride around in the open air, away from the critical eyes of the judges. I was more and more in love with Copperplate every day. She was a sweet, kind mare and surefooted and reliable when it came to jumping. Charles was riding his beloved Secret, and Janet was once again girding her loins and jumping Firestorm. I was surprised to see Lettie mounted on Jill's horse Balius. He was much taller than her own mare, at least two hands higher, but she had long legs and was sitting up straight and confident. What was much more surprising was Patrick mounted on a thickset grey horse that belonged to Mark Lansdowne.

"How did you get to cadge a ride on one of Mark's horses?" asked Charles, who wasn't one to hold back.

"I'm probably going to be leasing him for six months," mumbled Patrick, looking embarrassed.

Jill was staring at him, her eyes flashing angrily. Patrick saw her look and went bright red. He must have known that this was going to cause trouble. Perhaps, he wasn't sure exactly how it would upset Jill, but he sensed that there was bad blood between her and Mark.

"Which is this horse you're on, Jill?" asked Charles.

She swallowed down her anger and managed to answer him politely.

"He's Shadow. He's only been broken in lately. He's the full brother of my Balius, who Lettie is kindly riding around the course this afternoon."

"How are we going to arrange the jumping?" asked Charles. "Will it be an impromptu competition, or we all just go around and suit ourselves."

"I think we should ride around and look at the course, then we can get to know the track, and you can think about which jump you want to take. Most of them are three levels, and you choose what height or level of difficulty you want to tackle," said Jill.

The first jump was a log pile, inviting and easy. Even the highest version of it looked simple, perhaps only three-feet high.

"Can we just have a few goes at this one now?" asked Charles, who was inclined to be impatient.

"I don't see why not. Let's follow each other over the easy one; make sure they don't trip. It's so small."

We set off in a line. Charles went first with Secret, then Patrick flew it on Archer. Janet was struggling to hold Firestorm together. He was bursting out of himself and didn't like to wait for the others, he wanted to be at the front . Lettie flew over it easily on Balius, I followed on my darling Copperplate, who was as smooth as whipped cream, and then Jill on Shadow, who was manfully acting as if he had done this all his life.

Next was a series of three post-and-rails on a slight uphill slope with a narrow but deep ditch in front of them.

"Come on, let's all have a go over the lower one," shouted Charles, taking charge in his enthusiasm.

Secret leapt about twice as high as was needed. She seemed a little unsure of fixed cross-country jumps. Patrick followed on the deadly accurate Archer, and then Firestorm, plunging and snorting, raced towards it, went to stop dead, but pushed on by Janet, he catapulted himself over. She was a good rider, but she only just stayed in the saddle. Lettie and I flew together side by side as if we were practising for pairs. I realised that Copperplate and Balius had been stable mates and travelling companions for some time, and they got on very well together. Jill followed us with Shadow, anxious to keep up with the other horses. He leapt too early and slightly rapped it with one of his hind hoofs.

"That should teach you to be more careful," said Jill to him, giving him a pat and craning her head around to see if he had hurt himself. She trotted him in a straight line, but there was no unevenness in his movement.

"The next one is based on the Vicarage Vee, which is a famous jump at Burghley. The easy version of it is relatively simple, just an arrowhead with no ditch beneath it, but the middle part is much more difficult, it is the arrowhead wider, with the ditch beneath it, and the hard part, a very widespread with the deep and wide ditch beneath it. So I would suggest most of us will want to jump the easier bit to start with and have a good look at it if you want to have a go at the medium level difficulty."

I looked at the middle and difficult parts that looked terrifying. We all jumped over the easy bit quite smoothly, although Firestorm seemed to veer towards the difficult end at the last moment, and Janet only just managed to keep him straight.

The Normandy Bank, which for those horses that enjoy a slippery slide, was fun.

"Remember to lean well back," called Jill. She plunged ahead, pushing Shadow to do it alone without getting a lead. He tittupped at the lip of the bank, and it was only with some very vigorous leg aids that she kept him straight. He plunged down and then jumped when only halfway down. Jill wrapped her lower leg around the girth and leaned well back, letting the reins slip through her fingers. Secret wasn't at all sure that she liked this jump, and Charles let Patrick go on the robot-like Archer and followed on his tail. The rest of us managed to scramble down, a bit higgledy-piggledy, but we all made it safely to the bottom.

The Sunken Road was a jump down onto a lower level, a couple of strides, and then up and over a pole on the other side set high in the bank. The horses seemed to find this quite easy, and even Firestorm jumped it without any dramas. Then were the Barrels and the Garden Seat. None of them at the lowest level presented many difficulties, although again, Firestorm kept veering towards the higher end of everything.

The next jump was a series of three stiles, each separate from the other and all leading into a small dark copse. Patrick gave us a lead with Archer, who looked to neither right nor left, and jumped exactly where he was placed. Secret, who seemed to have palled up with the big solid grey, followed him, leaping about twice as high as necessary, and Charles knocked his knee against the side of the jump. It was his good leg, not his bung one, but it looked like it hurt. His face went white as a sheet. Lettie and I negotiated it successfully, but Janet and Jill decided to go around. Shadow wasn't nearly experienced enough, and Firestorm was so troublesome that Janet probably decided it wasn't worth having an accident.

Then was a tree trunk, balanced in such a way that it was above the ground. Hence, there was no groundline. Patrick set off and galloped up to it and over. He seemed to be gaining confidence with Archer and looked as if he were enjoying himself. Secret and Charles followed, and this time Secret appeared to judge the height more accurately and didn't leap too high. Copperplate and Balius set off after him, and Lettie and I jumped together. Firestorm was hot on our heels, and Janet took the liberty of kicking him on, daring him to misbehave. Jill pushed on Shadow, who looked at the obstacle and obviously decided that it wasn't too weird and jumped it boldly and confidently.

"He's going to be a good horse," said Janet.

"I think you're right," agreed Jill.

The picture frame was the last jump. It was very unusual. A large wooden frame that one jumped right through the middle. It was all one height and only about two feet. The sides were solid and very tall, and a single post was across the top. Although the idea of jumping through, rather than over, was kind of scary, it would be almost impossible for the rider to hit their head, no matter how high the horse jumped. All the horses galloped through one after the other.

"Now, I know it feels like we've been right around a course, but that was just the warm up," said Jill.

Susan rode up.

"Am I too late?" she asked.

"No, not at all. We're all going to go round once. You can follow me if you like," said Charles.

"Perhaps Susan should follow Archer. I think both Tranquil, and he are up for the highest jumps." You might like to stick to the low ones," said Jill bossily.

Charles looked a bit put out but could see the reasoning behind this idea.

"I'm going to go for the middle jumps. What about you, Rennie?" said Lettie.

"I'll go for the middle jumps as well," I said. I might even have had a shot at the highest, but my cautious nature kicked in, even though I did feel buoyed up with confidence.

"I think Shadow has had enough for one day," said Jill.

"So have I," said Janet, "more than enough! I'm going to take Firestorm back to the stables now, go in, have a nice cup of tea, and treat myself to a plate of Cook's goodies." She dismounted then, as if to prove her point, and led the big chestnut horse back down towards the stables.

"I'm glad I don't have to ever ride that horse," I said quietly to Lettie.

"I wouldn't mind having a try on him in the indoor school," she said, "but not jumping and certainly not jumping out here around the cross-country. There's a limit to just how much experience one should experience!"

"Susan, maybe you should trot and canter around a bit to warm up Tranquil," called Jill. "Now, what order are we going in? Perhaps Archer, then Tranquil, Copperplate, Balius, then Secret. Does everyone agree? Alright. I'll set you off at three-minute intervals."

Patrick trotted a few circles on Archer and shouted out.

"I'm ready to go now!"

"Go!" shouted Jill in response. "Susan, ready in three minutes."

Susan looked a little flustered, but she must have done cross-country courses a hundred times throughout her pony club career.

"Go!" shouted Jill, and she set off.

"Rennie, you're up next," said Jill.

Then I was off and flying. Copperplate was the most wonderful confidence-giving horse, and I wished above all else that I might be able to take her home. I was momentarily distracted by the sight of Patrick and Archer flying over the suspended tree trunk, but then I fixed my eyes on each jump and didn't think about anything else. We leapt over the first logs, then the middle post-and-rails with the ditch. I had thought the Vicarage Vee might be the hardest, but with Copperplate cantering briskly, we approached and were over before I could even feel nervous. I enjoyed the slide down the bank. Then we popped down onto the sunken road, two strides and up out. The barrels presented no problems, nor the garden seat. I gathered up the reins and rode as accurately as possible towards the middle of the stile, through the small copse, and then when we came back out into the open we gathered pace to go over the tree trunk, popped through the picture frame, and it was all over. I felt a rush of pure exhilaration. That was glorious, a piece of heaven on earth.

I turned and saw Lettie on Balius galloping in behind us. She must have been faster, riding all out as if it were a true competition. I watched Secret gallop over the tree trunk through the picture frame at an angle. Charles was looking pretty excited as he came in.

"By gosh, that was fun! Absolutely mustard! I think I'm going to be converted to one-day eventing!" he cried.

We rode back down the hill to the stables chattering away. Each of us retelling our round and extolling the virtues of our horses. The camaraderie between us overtook any competitiveness we might have felt trying to win the weekend in Vienna.

PART EIGHT
by Linda Gillis

Chapter Fifteen

The hardest part of running this two-week event for the prize winners was to prepare them to give lessons to my riding school pupils. Although each of the prize winners was an able rider and had certainly had instruction of one type or another, in some cases a great deal of teaching, I wasn't happy about it. I guess I was very possessive about my students. I had been running my riding school single-handedly for several years on a small unprepossessing patch of land I had inherited from my grandfather. Only recently, my small business had been incorporated into the larger newly-established enterprise of Blainstock Stables.

It wasn't just moving from my small premises, running my own show to the much grander facilities of Blainstock Castle, but also marrying Hugh Gillis. We were now invested in a future that was not entirely within our control but mixed up in the complicated finances of Blainstock Stables and an even more complex network of strong personalities.

The stables were barely surviving from week to week, and we were entirely dependent on the income from the riding school students. There were big plans of taking horses on livery, training for other people, bringing on our own horses and competing on them to sell for a profit, but so far none of this had come about. Hugh and I did our best to hide our genuine fears that this enterprise was going to fall into a black hole of insolvency. We kept our traps shut and put in our best effort to keep it going.

I had sold my property which consisted of a small scrap of land, a tiny cottage and lots of outbuildings that had been used as stables. I had suggested to Hugh that I should invest this money in Blainstock, but he had declared, point blank - 'absolutely not'. He said that money was my only security, and anyway, I had contributed a great deal to the stables with all my riding ponies and horses and tack, and I did more than my fair share of the work. He didn't add that Jill, who was a quarter owner of this new business, was a flibberty gibbet, dashing off to Australia for a holiday and heading down south to Oxfordshire whenever she felt the need for a change of scene. We were too loyal to say these things out loud, but I know that we both thought them.

The fourth member of our business co-operative was John, who had previously been the groom at Blainstock. He was a very reliable worker and also a steady, decent chap. We knew we could always rely on him. He uncomplainingly doled out feeds, stuffed hay nets, scrubbed and filled water buckets, mucked out stables, groomed horses, tacked up, cleaned saddlery, let out horses in paddocks and brought them in, changed rugs, took horses out for exercise, and the hundred and one other jobs that are involved in running a stable.

Even before the business had started, Jill had created an enormous problem. She had been needling Mark Lansdowne and had offered him livery for his other horses in exchange for Firestorm. It had been a mad offer. Firestorm was a magnificent-looking horse, but he had a difficult temperament and never looked like becoming an asset. So now, we were stuck with £5,000 worth of livery that we had to supply, and we were feeding Firestorm, a horse that no one would ever want to buy for that price.

We had given him to Janet Fawley to ride this fortnight, and she was managing him remarkably well, but she was an exceptional rider. I had thought we might be able to take him down south this summer and compete, perhaps sell him. But Hugh and I were needed at the castle for the summer visitors and that would mean sending him down with Jill. She was a good rider but not brilliant. I wasn't sure that she would be able to ride him to win and then negotiate a good sale. It was a conundrum, entirely of Jill's making, and Hugh and I had gone around and around the problem and not come up with an answer.

And, it wasn't just Blainstock Stables, but also the castle business that wasn't prospering. Hugh had been talking to Richard, and bookings for this summer were very few. The British were going abroad these days instead of to Scotland. The Continent had become more accessible and was luring the tourists to hot sunny beaches that looked over the azure-blue sea in the south of France, Italy and the Greek islands. The pasty white Britishers were delighting in lying in the sun and turning lobster red.

On Sunday afternoon, after all the organising of my riding school students being taught by the prize winners, I was utterly exhausted, more from nervous tension than actual physical activity. Hugh insisted I take some time off, and he sent me to the castle to have tea with Catherine. She was a wonderful woman and had a soothing effect on my tattered nerves.

We were happily ensconced in the library. After sipping Darjeeling from china teacups and nibbling on gingerbread, I flung myself on the rug playing horsey rides with Hamish, when the telephone rang. I clambered to my feet and picked it up as Catherine was hiding behind an armchair making neighing noises. I could hear the beeps of a long-distance call, and then an operator with an American accent was asking if that was Blainstock Castle. I replied that yes, it was.

This call was to change our fortunes for good and ill. I gestured to Catherine that she should take it. She extricated herself from chubby Hamish, who had found her behind the armchair, and took the receiver that I was holding out to her. I could only hear her end of the conversation, and I earwigged shamelessly.

"Hello."

…..

"How do you do? Yes, my name is Catherine Micheldever."

….

"I see. Well, certainly we have a house that we would be able to rent to you. Yes, it is called the Dower House and has five bedrooms, two bathrooms, a full kitchen and a scullery, a large drawing room, and a dining room. I'm sure that it would be more than adequate for three adults. Yourself, your husband and your trainer, you said."

….

"How long a lease are you after? Is it just for this summer?"

…

"A year. That would be absolutely satisfactory. There really is no need to pay in advance, but if you insist."

I could see her eyes lighting up with hope. The tired worried lines etched at the corners of her eyes seemed to vanish.

…

"Privacy? I think I know what you mean. The Scottish Highlands are quite remote. I mean, we do have guests who come up in the summer to shoot the grouse, but if you were in the Dower House, then there would be no reason for mixing with them. Unless, of course, you wished to join in with the social activities, in which case you would be very welcome."

….

"The stables. Yes, you're quite right. We have an indoor school, two cross-country courses, an outside showjumping arena and stabling for a large number of horses. Would you be bringing your own horses with you?"

....

"Oh, I see."

....

"You've heard of Skydiver? Goodness, I had no idea that he was that well known. He's hardly competed in England yet. How extraordinary!"

....

"That is, to say the least, a very tempting offer. But, of course, it will be up to my daughter, Jill Crewe. He is her horse. Do you have a phone number where I can contact you?"

...

"Oh, I see. If you would like to arrange with your bank to wire the rent money, we can expect you within a week. We'll make sure that the Dower House is prepared for you, and you can talk to Jill when you get here."

She hung up the phone, and I looked at her with lifted eyebrows. She was dazed.

"That was the most extraordinary phone call I think I have ever received," she said.

"I couldn't help hearing your end of it. Does this mean that you're renting out the Dower House?" I asked, agog with curiosity.

"It's not just that. They want to buy Skydiver and have offered £20,000!"

"He's a brilliant horse, but he can't be worth that much!" I exclaimed. "How on earth did they know about him anyway? It's not like he's achieved international fame!"

"She said her husband had seen him while living in the United Kingdom. Her husband is British, and they're coming over here this week. I know that Jill gave a dressage exhibition at Chatton Show. Perhaps he was there and saw her? They wanted somewhere secluded to live. It sounded almost as if they were on the run. They must be horsey people as they said they were bringing their horse trainer."

"Who travels the world with their horse trainer in tow!" I asked.

"This American woman. Although, she sounds very young, almost a child. I must go and find Richard and tell him."

"Do you think Jill will agree to sell Skydiver?" I asked.

"I don't know. But it would certainly solve some financial problems if she did!"

"I'll stay here with Hamish, and you can go and find Richard," I said.

She left the room, and I sat staring into the fire. It all seemed too good to be true. A bolt from the blue that might save all our fortunes. Perhaps the whole thing was a hoax.

The news that we had rented out the Dower House for twelve months buzzed around the stables. Even the prize winners picked up on the news. But we had decided to keep the offer to buy Skydiver a secret.

Hugh and I had stayed up long into the night discussing this turn of events. It was good news for the castle, but the stables' finances were a separate issue. Even if Jill agreed to sell Skydiver, we would be no better off as he belonged to her personally. We would benefit from the Americans paying for the livery of Skydiver, and perhaps they would buy other horses, but this was not going to be enough to put the equestrian business on a sound economic footing.

"Well, at least if they buy Firestorm, it will solve a few problems," I suggested.

"Certainly, but I don't think that's likely. He's the sort of horse that everybody admires but no one wants to deal with."

"What do you think of Mark arranging for young Patrick to lease Archer?" I asked.

"Mark is quite sharp when it comes to survival," replied Hugh. "In the short term, the boy can't harm the horse, and it means he'll be down south ready for Mark to pick up and compete in the autumn horse trials."

"Jill will be fuming over Mark scoring points over her," I said thoughtfully.

"Let's hope she doesn't come up with another scheme that will totally destroy the finances of the stables," said Hugh grimly.

"They're arriving on Wednesday, so we'll soon find out how it's going to work out," I said.

"Overshadowing the grand finale of the prize winners' competition," said Hugh.

"Life is moving on apace," I mused. "We'll just have to wait and see how it pans out."

Chapter Sixteen

On Monday morning, it was all hands on deck. Catherine and Hugh had gone over to the Dower House with a gaggle of young women from the village to scrub and clean. John was roped in to repaint some of the window sills. Hugh was oiling hinges and running taps and wondering if he should call in a plumber.

Despite the excitement at the imminent arrival of the Americans, Jill and I had to carry on with the prize winners' schedule. All the competitions would be finished by Tuesday night. Then there would be the announcement of the winner, followed by three days of recreational activities, including riding to the sea, and an impromptu cross-country competition.

Rennie was to do her dressage test on Skydiver on Monday after lunch, and Lettie would do hers' on Tuesday. I spent an hour training Rennie on Monday morning while Jill took the others to the showjumping arena so they could spend some time schooling over fences. Rennie was nervous when she mounted Skydiver, but he didn't react. He was a remarkable horse and seemed to go out of his way to reassure her. I explained the aids for the more advanced movements, and she practised them. Once she had mastered the sequence of transitions, she gained confidence and rode very well. If she had been just a little more self-confident, she could have come on in leaps and bounds, but she lacked that burning ambition, competitiveness and belief in herself that marked out the top riders.

I let her ride through her test just once. On principle, this wasn't a good idea, but I felt the benefits of bolstering her up were greater than the danger that Skydiver might remember the test and pre-empt her aids. He had been doing such a range of diverse tests since the prize winners had been riding him that I wondered if he would ever remember one particular sequence of movements for the rest of his life.

I hadn't discussed the arrival of the Americans with anyone except Hugh. So it was up to Catherine and Richard to talk to Jill about it. I was curious as to her view on selling Skydiver, but I was loathed to get involved. Ever since we took over the stables, I was very careful in discussing things with Jill these days. I felt that she couldn't be trusted.

Mark and Mercedes did not arrive until after lunch on Monday. They were not overly friendly with the prize winners, and I felt they resented having to be the judges. I wondered if they were being paid or had been persuaded to carry out their duties merely for the publicity they might receive.

Mercedes was the type who engaged in good works, but I had known Mark for years, and he didn't do anything if there wasn't a tangible reward for him in the offing.

I helped Rennie mount in the stable yard and reassured her that she would do well. I watched from the sidelines, and I was pleased with her performance. I hoped that her marks would reflect her success. Of all the prize winners, she was the one who needed the most encouragement. She was nervous, but Skydiver carried her through very creditably. Perhaps he was worth the exorbitant sum of £20,000.

On Monday night, we had the competition for assembling the double bridle. The prize winners had known about it for a while, and I had seen Lettie and Patrick practising in the tack room. Unfortunately, we only had three double bridles as none of us was much for showing. Two of them were Jill's, which she had used with her ponies Black Boy and Rapide, and there was an old one that Mark had used in his junior days.

We would run two heats, and each of the competitors would be timed. There was a lot of banter before the competition. Janet, Patrick and Susan were in the first heat. The other three prize winners were cheering them on, although perhaps the cries from the spectators were designed to distract them. It had been agreed that Hugh, John and I, with a stopwatch each, would time them and that Mercedes and Mark weren't needed. Patrick was the fastest, Janet came in second, with Susan miles behind, having cheerfully got into a tremendous muddle. All three of us checked the bridles to ensure they had been put together correctly. None of the times was announced. Then it was the turn of Rennie, Lettie and Charles. Rennie and Lettie were neck and neck, and Charles came in a distant third. Again, we examined the bridles, and each was correctly assembled.

"Now, we're going to announce the winners and the times," I said.

"First with the fastest time was Patrick. Well done, Patrick!"

Everyone cheered and clapped enthusiastically.

"Second was Janet, third was Lettie, fourth was Rennie, and fifth was Charles."

"I'm nowhere," moaned Susan with a mock-sorrowful expression.

"Well, I'm second last, so we shall just have to comfort each other," said Charles in a brave attempt at gallantry. Obviously, his adoration of Susan hadn't waned over the last week. He was just as smitten as he had been upon first setting eyes upon her.

There was a lot of scrabbling around with scraps of paper and pens as they tried to work out the scores so far. There were still the points for jump building and dressage to go, so it was no real indication of the final scores. We left them to it and went and did the final checks on the horses.

Lettie was to do her dressage on Skydiver tomorrow, and we had decided that if the weather was good, the others could go out on a long ride across the moor with John. We thought they might all have had enough of indoor schooling, and it was a waste if they didn't get to enjoy some of our glorious Scottish countryside.

Then, there would be judging of the jumps in the late afternoon. Tomorrow night Mark and Mercedes would attend a presentation, the winner would be announced, and photos would be taken. Bevan would leave on Wednesday morning, and Mark and Mercedes would not be returning to Blainstock. So the prize winners would have time to relax and enjoy themselves. For Hugh and me, the arrival of the new tenants of the Dower House was looming on the horizon. We were conscious that it could be fantastic for all of us, or in the worst of situations where we had to put up with the continual presence of some very demanding and arrogant guests.

The following day I was sorting out who was to ride which horse out on the loch. Janet had begged to be allowed to ride any horse but Firestorm. She admitted to me that she was sure he had been such a challenge that she had gained oodles of experience, but she was looking forward to enjoying a pleasant ride over the hills. I agreed with her. She had certainly done the hard yards with Firestorm. However, he was almost an impossible horse, and no one in their right mind would choose to buy him. So I suggested Balius, who was sufficiently schooled and experienced, to be an enjoyable ride. Despite his size, he had been born and bred up here and was very sure-footed on the mountain tracks.

Patrick had decided that his first loyalty must be to Scarlet Pimpernel, and he didn't want to risk Archer falling on his knees on the rocky tracks and injuring himself. Susan said that she did fancy Cammie, who was such a pretty horse, and Charles agreed to ride Jester, the other riding school horse who was often paired with Cammie. Rennie stuck with the reliable and sweet-tempered Copperplate, and John rode Shadow, who was still a novice and needed as much riding as he could get.

Hugh told me that Richard had suggested that the two of them get together to have a business discussion. I was inquisitive as to what might be the subject of such a talk. Still, I had to give Lettie her private lesson on Skydiver, and I would learn soon enough if there were any new developments concerning the arrival of our guests from America.

Lettie and I went to the indoor arena. I was surprised to see how well she handled Skydiver. He was a big horse, and she was only fourteen years old, but I could see that she showed great promise. Perhaps of all the prize winners, she was the one that might go far if she had the right opportunities and, of course, a big dollop of luck. I knew she had been taught to ride by the famous Frenchman, Pierre St Denise, but I hadn't focused on her before. She had a wonderful seat. No matter how hard one trains, a good seat is a gift from the gods. She also had very light hands. There was no pulling the horse together as one often sees in people attempting the noble art of dressage.

I helped her to work on her transitions so they were spot on and accurate, occurring as Skydiver's shoulder passed the marker. She listened attentively and responded to every suggestion I made. I even got her to attempt a levade, which was a rear in ordinary horseman's language. She made a very creditable effort.

Mercedes and Mark came over, and she did her test on Skydiver. I was disappointed. She missed some of the transitions by a stride or two, and her two-tempi flying changes were a little inaccurate with three canter strides before the change, but I could see heartening potential there. It did inspire me.

I seemed to have got so mired down in my riding school students and making a profit, not to mention my wedding to Hugh, that I had forgotten my attempts to climb to the top of the competitive equestrian world. Perhaps, I should start making my own riding career more of a priority. Hugh and John were more than capable of running the riding school if I got a chance to go further afield and compete. The most critical issue that had to be organised was finding myself a truly good prospect to compete on. I had never really felt like Skydiver was for me. He was indubitably Jill's horse, and if anyone was going to ride him to glory, then it would be her. Shadow had all the makings of a good horse but didn't have that star quality that could take a rider to the top. We had three ex-racehorses left out in the field, and we were to start work on them shortly. I sighed a little at this. It wouldn't be the first time I'd started from scratch with a horse that had raced and picked up a hundred bad habits along the way. As soon as the horses I trained competed, I was forced to sell them to keep going. Now, I resolved not to forget my own ambitions. I would talk to Hugh. He had been hinting for some time that I needed to put myself first instead of pouring myself out for everyone else. I knew that he would support me.

The prize winners had taken sandwiches with them and weren't returning for lunch. So after lunch, I sat down with Mercedes, and we went through the dressage tests. I was interested in the comments that she had written about each rider. She was smart and had made pertinent points about how each rider might improve. I thought it would have been good if she had given me some advice, but it was not the time to ask.

The riders would be clattering back into the stable yard, and I went over to help unsaddle and settle the horses. The prize winners were to set up their jumps in the indoor arena, and there would be the final bout of judging. It had been decided that after the jump judging, Jill would take Copperplate over the jumps. We had thought that this was the safest course of action. The pretty mare was the most reliable jumper. Firestorm might have charged through the middle of them, smashing them to bits. Balius was not very experienced, and he might just have thought them too weird and swerved away.

Susan and Charles' dragon was a magnificent creature and would make a wonderful centrepiece in any showjumping competition that we might hold in the future. Lettie and Rennie's wall was very artistic, and they might even find a place to put it in the castle's garden as an ornament. Janet and Patrick had put in minimum effort for their jump, but it would not have been a disgrace at Hickstead. It was rather an obvious first, second and third in that order.

Mercedes and Mark walked around each jump, paying close attention to the construction, how it would be jumped, and how it might come apart if it were hit. They didn't skimp on this last piece of judging which I thought was probably down to Mercedes' professionalism. Mark was looking restless as if he couldn't wait to get away.

There was no announcement over which jumps had won. That would come later in the evening. We were attempting to build the tension for the grand prize giving tonight. Jill galloped into the ring on Copperplate and did a few circuits with a flourishing touch of showmanship. Bevan was clicking away with the camera. Copperplate's mane and tail had been plaited, and she did look beautiful, gleaming chestnut and neat little shiny black hoofs. They jumped each of the obstacles, leaping clear. Then around and over again and everyone clapped like mad. Jill doffed her cap with a grin stretched across her face. Anyone would think she had won the grand prize herself.

We were all frocking up for dinner tonight. I decided that I would wear my wedding dress. It was an unfussy cream silk sheath to which had been attached a modest train. I took off the train and wondered how I might dress up my outfit. In the end, I went up to Catherine's bedroom to see if she had any ideas.

"Oh, darling Linda, with your lovely, elegant poise, you would look good in a sack but let's think what we might add to give a bit of colour," she said, looking at the dress, which I had laid out on her bed. "It's only a few months since your wedding, but it feels as if it were an age ago. You know we could go traditional Scottish and give you a tartan sash with a silver clasp."

"I don't have a sash of Hugh's tartan, and I can't wear that of another clan. It would be disrespectful," I said uncertainly.

"Here is just the thing!" announced Catherine, who had been burrowing through one of her drawers. She waved a bright silk shawl, coloured yellow, red and turquoise. We can drape this around your dress. I'm not sure how. Put it on, and we'll try it and see what we can come up with."

I slid into the dress, and Catherine fussed around, trying this and that.

"There, I think I've got it! Have a twirl in front of the mirror and tell me what you think. You look as exotic as a tiger lily in a bed of white daisies."

I twisted from side to side and was quite amazed at the effect. Catherine had successfully transformed me into a vision of bright, glamorous beauty.

"You're a miracle worker!" I exclaimed.

"Alright, darling, off you go. I must get my glad rags on to make it a grand evening tonight."

I went down to the library, and Mercedes was there. She had also dressed up, wearing a gorgeous crimson and dark blue taffeta. The dress looked like it had cost her a million pounds, and she wore it so casually it might have been a cotton summer frock. What it must be to have grown up wearing only the best and mixing with the highest people in the land.

We assembled in the drawing room. Richard and Hugh were busy behind the bar concocting drinks for everyone. There was a pervading air of gaiety and excited anticipation. Bright chatter flashed around the room.

We filed into the dining room and ate our way through two courses. The presentation was to take place before dessert was served. Glasses were charged with fizzy white wine, and Richard tapped his glass with his knife and called us to order.

"I'm not going to make you wait on tenterhooks. Let's get right down to it. First, I will announce the marks awarded for the dressage test. Then Mark will tell us the placings in the jump construction competition, and Mercedes will announce the overall winner who is off to the Spanish Riding School for a weekend."

The top scorer in the dressage is Janet Fawley, followed by Lettie Lonsdale, Susan Barington-Brown, Patrick Huntingdon and Rennie Jordan.

"I can't believe it," squeaked Susan, "I'm third."

"Of course, you are," countered Charles robustly, "you're a jolly good rider."

I was pleased that Lettie had come second. Despite her obvious mistakes, she had gotten the best out of Skydiver. I didn't suppose that Charles would be too upset to be last, he was the least experienced of all the riders, and dressage was not his thing.

"Oh, well done, Janet! You deserve it," said Patrick smiling at her.

Mark got to his feet and called for order.

"The best jump constructed was the dragon by Susan and Charles, followed by the landscape wall painted by Lettie and Rennie, and last but not least, the decorative hogsback by Janet and Patrick," he said and sat down abruptly.

Everyone clapped and cheered, and then there was some frantic calculation. No one knew how the jump marks would be awarded, so no one could foretell the final winner. Mercedes stood and held up her hand. She looked very regal as if she were royalty. A hush fell over the table.

"Without further ado, as they say in these types of speeches, I would like to announce the prize winner with the top score, who wins the weekend in Vienna, is (she paused for two dramatic seconds) Janet Fawley."

A tremendous burst of clapping greeted this announcement. Everyone liked Janet, and it was unanimously agreed that she deserved to win.

"I've got a small trophy here for you, Janet, if you would like to come up and receive it," went on Mercedes.

Janet stumbled to her feet. She was very red in the face. She walked around the table, and everyone was cheering her on and shouting their congratulations. Mercedes handed her the trophy, and Bevan's camera flashed, and the moment was preserved to go down in history.

I felt a wave of anti-climax. Hugh and I had put so much work into this event, and now it was over. I was sure that it would be deemed a success, and I hoped that the article that Bevan was writing would do Blainstock justice and attract more business. It had not been a cheap endeavour, but hopefully, it would be worth it.

PART NINE
by Jill Crewe

Chapter Seventeen

I have been waiting for my turn to write this story, dying of impatience to have my say. I'm not good at staying in the background, which I'm sure my faithful readers will know. In fact, if you read my books, you may be under the impression that drama lurks in every corner of my life. It is just, like soap operas, I pick out the high points of adventure and intrigue and do not describe all the mundane everyday realities of meals, housework, dressing, undressing, brushing my teeth, writing thank you letters to aunts and every other sort of mindless task that makes up a large portion of civilised human existence.

When it came to this fortnight of entertaining the prize winners, there had been a series of high points. It is always interesting to bring together a group of people who do not know each other. There is the constant quest to find points of connection and establish new alliances, with the added spice of rivalry, pique and ignoble jealousy.

I must say I was thrilled that Janet Fawley won the grand prize as she was probably the least likely, along with Rennie, to be able to take herself off to the Spanish Riding School. The fact that she had invited Patrick to accompany her was entirely fitting. He had come a close second in the points, and they both deserved it! Not that there was anything romantic in this joint trip, unlike Charles and Susan, who had fallen in love at first sight.

All the prize winners, John and myself, are off to ride to the sea tomorrow. Hugh will go by road in the Land Rover and meet us there with a lovely selection of comestibles to be consumed, some hay for the horses and buckets of water. Mummy and Richard have to stay at the castle because some Americans are arriving to live in the Dower House. This was certainly a bolt from the blue, and I think it is God, or the Master of Fates, sending us some much-needed business to boost our fortunes. Apparently, they're horsey, and they will probably keep some horses at the stables, so that means we will all benefit. I must admit there is something a little uneasy about Mummy and Richard's attitude, but perhaps they're wondering how these year-long guests will impact all our arrangements. I don't really care, guests, tenants, horses on livery, and paying riders are all grist to the mill as far as I am concerned.

I have to say this fortnight has definitely been a SUCCESS, and I made sure to write copious notes in glowing terms for Bevan to use in his article. I even suggested to him that I do a first draft, but he said no, he was perfectly capable of doing it himself. I hope he does us justice, as it has been a huge effort. It cost us a good lot of dosh to provide them all with deluxe hospitality, but hopefully this will translate into lots of visitors to Blainstock in the future. As part of the deal, *Riding* magazine will run a half-page advertisement for us for the next six months.

Mummy, Richard, Hugh and Linda have been very worried about the business's finances. They have meetings in the dining room, constantly looking over the accounts and talking in grave tones with worried frowns. I know that I should involve myself in this activity, but after Australia and playing hostess to the prize winners, I feel like I have enough on my plate. I am wondering how to spend my summer, and I've thought that a trip down to Chatton with Skydiver, Balius and perhaps even Shadow might fill in the time nicely.

I know I should have told the story about my trip to Australia before writing this book, but it was massive. I mean massive! Just before I left, Mummy dropped a bombshell on me that my father was alive and living in Australia after having spent years in prison for manslaughter. Considering I had spent my childhood being told that he was dead, this was a shock of the first order. That is all I'm going to say at this moment. I have to write it up and will as soon as I finish this light-hearted story, and then I will reveal ALL. I promise. I will probably call it *Jill Goes Showjumping Downunder,* which will fit in with the equestrian theme. I can't resist giving you one big hint. My father is a reasonably accomplished horseman and now works with horses. The rest of that story will have to wait tantalisingly on the horizon of books-soon-to-be-published. I suppose it will be something else I should be doing this summer.

On Wednesday morning, the day that we were to ride to the sea, we were consuming a hearty breakfast. All the prize winners were seated at the table in dashing high spirits. Now that the competitions were over, the winner decided it was time to enjoy a ride in the fresh, clear Highland weather. They were such a lovely bunch of people. There was not a pompous ass, nor a know-it-all, or a sarky one amongst them. Charles was still making goo-goo eyes at Susan, who seemed perfectly happy to be the recipient of such treatment. Patrick was such a decent fellow, chatting to each of the others in turn. Janet was smart as a whip but without an ounce of side. Timid Rennie was obviously feeling more at ease, smiling, listening, and nodding. Lettie was as sharp as a little bird. She still seemed conscious of the fact that she was several years younger than the others, but she cut into the conversations every now and again with a clever comment.

Mummy called me aside after I had finished my plate of eggs, bacon and black pudding. With half an eye on the others, who were gulping down their cups of coffee about to depart, I asked her if it was urgent. She looked at me in a funny way. Perhaps she wanted me to stay at the castle and not take part in the ride across country. I must say this would be a drag. I was looking forward to going on a lovely outdoor jaunt and enjoying myself.

"You know these people that are coming today," said Mummy.

"Well, not really, a couple and their horse trainer who travels with them! I mean, who takes a horse trainer around the world with them?"

"They're talking about buying a few horses," said Mummy.

"Jolly good. Perhaps they might snap up Firestorm. Now that would be a relief for everyone!" I exclaimed.

"Perhaps . . ," said Mummy.

"Look, the others are going over to the stable yard. Can this wait until we get back?" I said, starting to walk away.

"Of course," she said in a strangled voice, and I didn't give it another thought.

I followed the others who were rushing out into the castle courtyard and round the path to the stables. The horses were all tacked up and waiting for us, and within five minutes, we were heading up the path between the small fields towards the loch. Janet looked content to be riding the placid Jester. I was mounted on Balius, marvelling at how good he was to ride these days. Lettie was on Martini, Charles on Secret, Susan on Tranquil, and Rennie on Copperplate. I had wondered if Patrick might ride Archer again, but he was mounted on Scarlet Pimpernel.

It was one of those perfect spring days. There was a pale, turquoise sky with a delicate tracery of cirrus clouds. The sunlight had more silver in it than gold, and its cool radiance was invigorating and promising.

It was one of those gilded days of unadulterated pleasure, riding through the wonderful countryside with a gaggle of worthy companions. We could see the mountain range on the horizon, the peaks lost in a sun-shot mist whose trailing veils screened the light. There was a purple haze of ling on the hills that rose above the loch, and we could smell the sweet scent of heather.

We followed a path around the rocky edges of the loch and then branched off and headed west through the hills. John had been riding this country all his life and led the way. He knew the best paths for the bigger horses who weren't as nimble on the rough ground. We came upon a tiny burn where the tinkling water pooled in a circular stone formation before spilling down the hill towards the loch.

"We could stop for a minute and let the horses have a few mouthfuls of this green grass," said John, full of cheer, turning around to speak to the riders behind him. Patrick's big bay horse had obviously never eaten grass with a bit in his mouth and a rider on his back. He looked around in bewilderment. Jester was an old hand when it came to trekking across the hills, and he put his head down and snatched up as much green grass as would fit in his mouth. Lettie's Martini had rather a crush on the handsome Jester, and she stood beside him and nibbled the succulent green grass. Balius, who had been born in the Highlands, knew the drill and took some big satisfying mouthfuls. He had gone to the sea before, and he knew that it was a long ride and he would need as much energy as possible.

We pushed on, trotting and cantering when it was possible. All the horses and ponies were fit and eager, and finally, we came to the beach. It was an ebb tide. Flights of gulls were patterning the sky, and waves were rippling onto the sand. The ponies' hoofs crunched beneath us on the fine, broken shells. They jumped across long tendrils of seaweed that lay strewn here and there.

"I wish it was warm enough to bathe!" shouted Rennie. "I've never ridden on a beach before."

"You need to come back in the summer," I said thoughtlessly, forgetting that Rennie's family circumstances meant that a holiday in the Highlands was probably far beyond their reach.

"You could come up one summer and work at the stables if you like, a sort of holiday job," I quickly added, hoping this wasn't too reckless an offer. I had to be careful not to propose things for the stables business without consulting the other three. I had learned my lesson with the Firestorm fiasco.

Hugh was parked in the Land Rover at the far end of the beach, and we rode up to him and dismounted. He had brought headcollars for each horse and had a couple of buckets that he filled with fresh water from some eight-gallon containers. He had some hay nets stuffed with meadow hay. We took turns holding the horses while they ate and drank. Cook had provided the usual wonderful spread, and we all ate voraciously. It had been a long time since breakfast.

After we'd eaten and the horses and ponies had munched their way through the hay nets, we set off back to the castle. The fresh air had filled our lungs, and our minds were blown clean with the good Highland air. It was one of those simple days of pure bliss that took me back to my childhood before I had had to struggle with the complexities of adult life, the worries of earning a living, and making my way in the world.

I was in a happy dream the time we arrived back at the castle. We rode down the path beside the small stone-walled fields. Balius had given me a good ride. He was much more balanced these days and not falling over his own hoofs. I was sure he was ready to shine this summer in novice jumping classes. There is nothing better in life than planning a summer season of the shows, especially when one has several horses that are ready to compete.

I must admit that I had put some of my more noble intentions to one side. Having taken off months on a jaunt to Australia, I had been determined that when I returned, I should put my back into the work of Blainstock Stables. Linda had done the lion's share of the work teaching her riding school kids, not to mention a major part of the instruction and organisation in the last two weeks. I thought I should pull my weight and show everyone that I was more than capable of undertaking honest toil. But when I set my mind to it, I could justify being lured down south this summer. I had to fly the flag for Blainstock, represent the stables, chalk up some victories, and perhaps try and get some business training other people's horses. Moreover, I could find a top-notch show pony for a reasonable price, and we could sell it to Mrs Frayne. That would be a win.

So satisfied was I with my lot after such a gilded day of indulgence that I decided I would make sure that my better self should triumph. I struck up a conversation with the blameless Patrick, asking him about his plans for Archer. I saw now that there was nothing wrong with Mark asking Patrick to take his horse for a six-month lease. I had to stop seeing dark motives in anything that concerned Mark. I even wished him well in his determined pursuit of Mercedes. She was undoubtedly a good rider, an attractive, even beautiful, woman and worthy in many ways, if a little less than entertaining. I had tried my best to crack her shell and really get to know her, but she was so remote. In the end, I concluded that she either has a very secret soul that she shields from the world, or she is an attractive package with no depths to plumb. Either way, she has a good influence on Mark and brings out the best in him. I believed that Mark was going to be invited to stay at Pevensy Park, he would propose, and if Mercedes accepted, then he would be made in the shade. He will get the girl and all the money in the world to follow his international three-day eventing career.

I was vaguely wondering what I should wear to the wedding. I couldn't see Mark managing not to invite me as I was his uncle's stepdaughter. I presumed it would be down in Oxfordshire. No doubt, there was a parish church which was in the living of Pevensy Park where Mercedes' people lived. Henry and Ann would be there as they were mixed up in that crowd, and of course, Susan Pyke, who was now Susan King, if she and her husband hadn't divorced by now as she had been running around with Mercedes' rackety brother, Austin. I mused on this strange conundrum that Susan should have married the boring Bartholomew King in the first place, then risked making herself so *declassé* as to become 'a bit on the side' for such a playboy. Then, we all clattered into the stable yard.

The sun was drawing reluctant golden fingers of farewell across the yard. This evening, the prize winners insisted on each tending to their own mounts. They had had enough of being pampered and waited upon, and now they wished to get back to doing things for themselves. I dismounted from Balius, gave him a good pat, unbuckled the girth, pulled off his saddle, sat it on one of the rails in the centre of the yard, and led him to his box. Linda came over and hung over the half-door while I was carefully taking his bridle off, making sure not to rip the bit through his teeth. Somewhere along the line, he had caught the bad habit of clenching his teeth around the bit when one was unbridling him.

"The new people have arrived and are riding Skydiver in the indoor arena now. Come on. You need to meet them. Jill, just a word of caution, you need to prepare yourself for this."

Foreboding flooded through me. The golden daze of the day dissipated. Something about the expression in Linda's eyes pierced through my happy dreams. I tried to hang on to the shreds of optimism. Why were they riding Skydiver? Perhaps, they were thinking of taking dressage lessons on him. But why did I 'have to prepare myself'?

Chapter Eighteen

I walked over to the indoor riding school, and there was a host of butterflies flapping around my stomach. My palms were dry, and my breathing shallow. I gave myself a bit of a talking to. The worst had to be that these people were awful riders and were going to ruin Skydiver, wrenching at his mouth and kicking him, and they were rich, and we needed their money, and we would have to put up with it.

I entered through the large double doors that were rolled back. A man was riding Skydiver. From a distance, he looked like a good rider. He had a ramrod straight back, his legs were bent in the correct position, and he held his hands steady in a slightly higher position than was used for normal riding.

Some lines from a poem by Eleanor Farjeon floated into my mind:

The wing on his shoulder

Was brighter than fire.

His tail was a fountain

His nostrils were caves,

His mane and his forelock

Were musical waves,

I felt uneasy. Where had this piece of poetry come from? I took a few stumbling steps closer to the man riding my horse. There was something familiar about him, something uncomfortably familiar. Skydiver passaged at the trot and then transitioned to the piaffe. A pirouette and he cantered on the spot. Then, without any visible aids, the man sent him at a floating extended trot around the arena.

"Oh, well done darling!" trilled a high-pitched American voice from a seat on the other side of the arena. Her accent would have to grate on anyone's nerves. I pulled myself together. I would walk over and introduce myself. I would do my bit for the business, putting on my friendliest face.

I edged around the side of the arena, not wanting to interrupt this rather splendid display of dressage. At least this man could ride! The woman was dressed flamboyantly, in the way that I guessed Americans usually dressed. She had a bright orange shirt with a flamingo-pink scarf tied around her neck. Her hair was brilliant yellow, carefully curled in an intricate style, and even from a distance, I could see her bright blue cornflower-coloured eyes.

"Good afternoon," I called cheerfully. I was now within a few yards of her, and I extended my hand in a friendly gesture.

"Oh, hello!" she said, beaming her piercing blue eyes towards me.

"I'm Jill Crewe, and that is my horse Skydiver," I said by way of introduction.

"Yola Laskey!" she announced, grasping my hand in a very firm handshake. Character must be measured by the strength of one's handshake in America.

"Laskey," I repeated, thinking that sounded so familiar, and then it came to me. The horrible dawning truth. I swivelled and looked at the man riding Skydiver. He was coming towards us with a big smug, sickly smile on his handsome face. It was Jack Laskey! This woman, Yola, was perhaps his young wife, a very young and obviously very rich wife. What had happened to his poor gormless fiancée Willow Vetch and her glamorous guardian, Belinda Bliss?

If you have read *Jill and the Horsemasters,* then you will know all about Jack Laskey and even worse, the enormous schoolgirl crush I had upon him. He was the embodiment of moral degeneracy, a rascal of the first order, and at the time, he had flattered me so that he could ride Skydiver, but then he had moved onto much richer pickings and got engaged to a young American girl, Willow, the daughter of the famous and very rich Bernie Vetch. I had been left licking my wounds and taking comfort in the fact that I had never declared my love to him. In fact, I had come to dislike him very much by the time he swanned off with Willow and Belinda to a life of luxury and top horses in America.

Now, here he was, married to quite a different young woman called Yola. Their horse trainer was skulking at the back of the group. He now stepped forward with a goofy grin.

"Hello, Jill," he said in an affable, casual voice as if he and I were old friends. Now, I really did gasp in surprise. It was Frank Stabley, a young man I had known nearly all my life, a showjumper from Chatton. Not that we actually had *history* in the true sense of the word, but he and I had gone out to dinner and shared a pizza some months ago. Then I had gone off to Australia, and he had gone to America to work with horses. Here he was!

I stood with my mouth open, gasping in what was undoubtedly a very unattractive manner.

"Remember, you sent me some brochures. I showed them to Jack and Yola when they were looking for a base in the United Kingdom; they thought this would be right for them. They're aiming to live a somewhat secluded life," he paused and then went on, "and then they will be competing. I remembered this magnificent horse, and Jack said he had ridden him, and he decided it would be a perfect wedding present for his new bride."

He was talking quite slowly and in a patient, explanatory manner. Obviously, I was gobsmacked, and he was giving me time to grasp the situation. By now, my face was the colour of beetroot.

"You're their horse trainer," I said slowly.

"Yes, they call me that. I'm travelling with them and helping them to find some good horses, and I guess I'm more of an assistant. It's not a permanent job, of course. But the thought of coming to Blainstock Stables and seeing you and where you live was more than I could resist."

Now, these words might have struck a romantic note in the heart of a young woman, delivered in such an earnest and honest way from such an estimable young man. But the juxtaposition of Frank, who was a real boyfriend possibility, and Jack, who had been a horrible and embarrassing crush, was too much for me. For some bizarre reason, I felt angry. As if I had been duped. Now, this was not at all reasonable. I supposed it was the shock.

Through the fog of my outrage and humiliation floated an echo of the words, 'a perfect wedding present for his bride'. They were talking about Skydiver! As if he were a glossy product displayed on the shelf of a shop for any ghastly rich person to take down and pay the price tag.

"So, Mr Laskey," Linda said in a cool, business-like tone, giving me a moment to gather my scattered wits.

"Do call me Jack," he said to her with a twinkle in his eye.

"What do you think of Skydiver?" she asked, for the moment ignoring his invitation to be on first name terms. "I understand that you have ridden him before."

"I think he is a stupendous horse. It is up to my darling wife if she likes him. Ultimately, it will be her choice," he replied.

I couldn't help myself. I was outraged.

"Her choice!" I was almost shouting. "I think I've missed something here! Since when has Skydiver been up for sale?"

Linda looked appalled. I stared at her as a dozen emotions flitted across her face.

"Jill," she hissed at me. "I wasn't sure what to do. We decided not to say anything until Jack and Yola arrived."

"Who is we?" I hissed back like a venomous snake as she took my arm and dragged me away.

"We must talk in private," she insisted, looking around wildly as if searching for someone else to help carry me away from a public debate that wouldn't go well.

"They said they wanted to buy Skydiver," she began.

"Oh, did they just?" I echoed, not bothering to lower my voice.

"We didn't know how they knew about him, but we thought we would leave it until they arrived. We didn't think it was worth worrying you if it wasn't going to come off. But you have to listen, this is important. I'm sorry we should have told you before. They're offering £20,000!"

Again, my mouth gaping like a goldfish, I tried to process this new information. Had she said £20,000.

"T – w – e – n – teeee," I squeaked.

"Yes, two nought, comma, nought, nought, nought," she replied, drawing circles in the air with her finger. "You must see what this might mean for us. They may even take Firestorm."

At the mention of Firestorm, I was pulled up short. The whole fiasco of buying Firestorm off Mark in exchange for £5,000 worth of livery was down to me. I had almost sunk the business before it started with my stupid mindless malice, taunting Mark.

"They can buy Firestorm," I said, attempting to be reasonable, "but Skydiver is *my* horse."

Linda looked at me helplessly. Later, when I began to think it over, I knew exactly what she must have been thinking. I was going to have to take one for the team. I was going to have to sell my precious dressage horse to save not only Blainstock Stables but also the castle, our family home. Everything now depended on me doing the right thing. The whole future of my family and colleagues hung on me being noble and selling Skydiver. And to *all* people, to Jack Laskey and his latest female conquest, who obviously adored him – and he had *married* her. I remembered comments made by the old guard about 'Johnny Foreigner', and I felt the first faint stirrings of xenophobia.

I was beginning to get a grip on myself when Frank, who seemed keen to see me, bowled over.

"How about we go out for another pizza!" he suggested.

The inanity of this comment drove me nuts. I was far beyond 'keeping my end up.' All reason slipped away on a tide of ill-feeling. I felt as if the whole universe was trying to ruin my life. That one date in my whole life led to this. I hadn't even wanted to dip my toe in the sea of romance, and now I was shipwrecked, dashing against the rocks of disloyalty.

I turned on my heel and marched away. I made my way to the castle, reduced to spluttering fury, incoherent thoughts churning through my brain. Did Mummy and Richard know about all this? They had to. Everyone had conspired to keep me in the dark. I was finding it hard to comprehend. I stumped up the stairs to my bedroom, which was situated in a turret, resolving that I would be like a princess, never to descend again due to the evil spell cast by those I had trusted.

I sat on my bed waiting for Mummy to come tapping on the door with all her usual tact and patience. She would apologise for what they had done and coax me downstairs. But no one came near me. I was going to have to wrestle with my demons and on an empty stomach.

I climbed out of my riding clothes and nestled down in my bed. I wasn't going to wash, change, or go down to dinner like an ordinary civilised person. I was in high dudgeon. Brooding darkly, I put the thought of Frank Stably aside and focused on Skydiver. I had taken a lot of trouble to acquire him. My fifth book, *Jill Dreams of a Dressage Horse*, tells the story of my quest to buy a dressage horse. At the time, I had felt that life would not be complete unless I had an absolutely top-notch dressage horse. I had acquired him a roundabout way, first off going on a quest to track down his owner and find out if he were for sale, and then getting together the money to pay for him. At the time I had considered it an exorbitant price, but nothing like £20,000.

Then the thought of that huge sum of magic money started to worm its way into my consciousness. I don't think that I'm a materialistic person, but the glorious power of money was waving itself tantalisingly in front of me. I had been thinking of my riding career, summers in Oxfordshire, and not bothering with the money worries that had beset Blainstock, both the castle and the stables. I had taken for granted my very own Pool Cottage, which my mother had gifted to me. The chance of having not one but two ponies in my childhood. My mother writing every day and night to pay the bills and give me things that other children had. With the money for Skydiver, I could help pay the bills for the castle for several years while we established the business. I could put more capital into the riding stables so that Linda didn't have to slave morning, noon and night. She deserved the chance to go out and compete.

As these thoughts rushed through my mind, I realised just how selfish I had been. It wasn't as if I even loved Skydiver, not in the way that I loved Black Boy and Balius. He had come to me a ready-made push-button dressage horse, and, somehow, I had never really connected with him on a spiritual level. He had taught me so much about what a truly high-class dressage horse was capable of, but my enthusiasm for the whole caper had waned. Perhaps, it was because in England, there really wasn't a proper dressage competitive scene. It was still a new activity. My first love was showjumping and always would be.

I remembered that we had found out the Skydiver could jump and that had opened up the possibility of high-level eventing with him. Jack Laskey didn't even know that Skydiver could jump; he had only ridden him as a dressage horse. Then I was overtaken by a capitalistic fervour that shook me, was he worth more than £20,000! I was learning more about the dark depths of my character than I could come to terms with in one day.

I decided that I would dress for dinner and go downstairs. I was ravaged with hunger and this encouraged me to seek sustenance. I had been behaving like a childish, spoilt brat, flouncing off like that. Then, I remembered Frank. Did I hate him for trying to sell my horse from under me, or was it all an elaborate ploy so that he could come to Scotland and pursue a romance with me?

Chapter Nineteen

I slid down the stairs. As I stepped into the hall, I could hear voices coming from the dining hall. I stopped to listen. There was the unmistakable simpering American voice of Lola.

"Oh Jack, darling, you know that you always lead me. You are the rider of the family." Obviously, any idea of feminism had entirely passed her by.

"Don't worry, my darling, you'll be the Queen of Dressage across the Continent," came the unmistakable deep chocolate and Cointreau tones of her husband.

Richard and Mummy must have glossed over my reaction this afternoon. It seemed as if the sale of Skydiver was going full steam ahead, with or without my say-so. How else would some upstart yank suddenly become the 'Queen of Dressage.' Quickly, I squashed down another childish outburst that was rising within me. I was going to prove once and for all that I was an adult, capable of making adult decisions.

I walked quietly across the hallway and stepped through the doorway that led to the long dining hall. I saw to my relief that my place was set, and I could slip into my chair easily without disrupting everyone's meal. They were still on the first course, so I wasn't too far behind.

"Sorry to be late," I murmured, seeing Mummy watching me out of the corner of my eye.

Yola Laskey kept talking, not noticing my entrance. She was clearly used to being the centre of attention, and nothing was going to stop her in full spate.

"I adore a top hat and tails. It looks like a costume for a Thanksgiving Parade."

The prize winners were sitting silently, agog at this line of conversation. Obviously, none of them had ever witnessed a Thanksgiving parade.

"Is that something like cheerleaders?" asked Rennie innocently, scraping the bottom of the barrel when it came to knowledge of American culture.

Frank was seated at the other end of the table, and I made sure not to catch his eye. I could only be thankful that Mark and Mercedes had left. The thought of Mark witnessing my humiliation would have made it unbearable.

The girl from the village who was serving tonight slipped a plate in front of me. It was pâté with little squares of toast and slices of smoked salmon decorated with radishes and carrots cut up to look like flowers. I tucked in and then slid my eyes around to look at Yola. When I had first met her, my attention had taken up with the garish colours of her garb, blonde hair and very blue eyes. Tonight, she was so scantily clad she was courting pneumonia. I averted my eyes from her acres of buxom young flesh and examined her features. Her eyes were large, her nose small and snub, and her thin lips painted a bright red. She had a very jutting-out chin that I thought might indicate that she liked to get her own way.

Jack was seated further down the table, and his expression was as oily and insincerely charming as ever. What a pair! They deserved each other. I wondered what had happened to Willow, the strange, drab, young woman with the egg-shaped head who had been engaged to Jack when I had last seen him. Obviously, he had traded her in for Yola, who was certainly more lively and self-confident, and presumably just as rich if they could afford to pay £20,000 for a horse without a second thought.

The main course was served, and I ate the thinly sliced roast beef with gravy and horseradish sauce, with Cook's best roast potatoes, sprouts, carrots and minted peas. It was delicious, and now I had gotten over my great wave of emotional upset, I set about assuaging my hunger. I noted that the prize winners had been rendered mute under the battering of Yola's self-confident barrage of patter.

A bitter mouthful of mean words was on my lips, but by a Herculean effort, I managed to slip in a rather sly question.

"How did you meet Jack?"

"Oh, that is such a story!" she began.

'You betcha it is,' I thought.

"We were at a horse show at Madison Square Garden, and he was sitting nearby. I could see him looking at me, and I refused to acknowledge him," she laughed coquettishly.

I wondered whether he had been there with Willow or her guardian, the impossibly glamorous Belinda Bliss. I was not so brazen as to ask. I could feel Jack looking at me, challenging me, but I ignored him.

"Have you been riding all your life," I asked, falling back on safe ground.

Jack gave me a smug smile.

"Oh yes, Daddy says I was born in the saddle," she tooted.

'How uncomfortable,' I thought.

"Is this your honeymoon?" I asked.

It was as if the world had been put on pause and the air sucked out of the night. The self-confident Yola baulked. I sensed blood and went in for the kill.

"I suppose you had a big society wedding?"

"It was more of a Gretna Green affair," said Jack conspiratorially. Yola smiled at him, her eyes darting a little here and there.

I would have to grill Frank to get the real story. Richard decided to throw the conversational ball in the opposite direction to steer away from this delicate topic.

"We hope that you are happy with the arrangements at the Dower House," he said.

"It's such a dinky little house," said Yola, as if she were used to living in a mansion. Perhaps she was.

"The riding around here is wonderful," said Mummy. "The Highlands is a very scenic area. The riders went all the way to the sea today. It takes two or three hours to get there."

"I'm looking forward to exploring the countryside," said Yola. "I'm from Virginia, which is quite a different landscape."

"What are the differences between horse riding in America, compared to England?" Janet asked Frank, smiling at him.

I looked at her suspiciously. Perhaps she was a bit too interested in Frank.

Dessert arrived in front of me; apple crumble served with cream and hot, steaming custard.

"They had a lot of different types of competition classes," said Frank helplessly, as if the differences were so huge and unusual that it was too big a topic.

"You must tell me all about it," said Janet, in her confident and friendly manner. My suspicions increased. She was obviously after him!

Mummy suggested that we all go into the library for coffee. She looked exhausted, as if we had been navigating a minefield. She looked at me meaningfully, in a way that suggested we needed a serious mother and daughter talk. I certainly wanted to ask her whether she had known that these people had wanted to buy Skydiver and why I had been kept in the dark.

Coffee was more relaxed as our guests were able to reconfigure themselves in small groups rather than stick to their appointed places at the dining table. Richard collared Jack, and they talked seriously about the Dower

House. Yola became the centre of attention amongst the prize winners. Although her first instinct was to talk about herself, she must have remembered her manners and begun to question them about the competition and what they had been doing. Of course, this led directly to them talking about how they had all performed an advanced dressage test on Skydiver. My claims to my dressage horse were looking less valid by the minute. I had to come to terms that he was not only going to be sold, but this would be flaunted under my nose every minute of every day while Yola and Jack rode him at Blainstock. My idea of going down to Oxfordshire began to look more attractive by the minute. I couldn't wait to escape. Except for Frank.

Eventually, Mummy managed to catch my eye, and she gestured that we should slip away. There was much to be said. We made our way to the kitchen where Cook and the girl were finishing the cleaning up.

"What did you know about selling Skydiver?" I asked, demanding to know.

"They rang up out of the blue," she replied. "They did mention Skydiver in that phone call, which was surprising. Linda was with me when I took the call, so she knew. I assume she would have told Hugh, and I told Richard. We agreed not to mention it to you as it seemed rather random, and we wanted to wait and see what happened when they arrived. It was unfortunate that you first heard of the possibility of them buying the horse when you met them. I remembered you mentioning a Jack who rode Skydiver at a dressage competition in Devon when you were away on that course at Porlock Vale."

"I see," I said, "but I still think that I should have been told. "That Jack Laskey! He was engaged to Willow Vetch the last time I had seen him. The poor girl had been abducted and rescued, and Jack saw his chance and swooped in. He was pretty tight with her guardian Belinda Bliss. Now, he's hooked onto this poor unfortunate Yola, who was obviously a better prospect."

"There does appear to be a bit of a mystery about their marriage," said Mummy. "I'm not sure that she's a 'poor unfortunate'. She seems to be very self-confident, a young woman who knows what she wants."

"My horse! And that Jack is as conniving as they come," I added.

"They seem to have come here to lie low for a while. But obviously, they've got money," said Mummy. "They've paid six months' rent into our bank account, and I'm assuming they've got the £20,000 for Skydiver. Did Jack have any money?"

"Not a penny, as far as I know," I said. "Although he might have got some money out of Belinda Bliss, being paid for his services," I added cattily. "But it's more likely that it's Yola's money. Perhaps she's the spawn of some mafia family, and they're after Jack for sweeping her away."

"Oh! Really, Jill! That's just too dramatic. Where do you come up with these things!" exclaimed Mummy, giving me an old-fashioned look. "But the real question is, are you willing to sell Skydiver?"

"I don't see that I have much choice," I said grudgingly. "We're desperate for funds, and it would certainly give us some money to keep going so that we don't lose the castle."

She sighed. I realised then how much the sale meant to her. I felt mean having had such a bad reaction. Thinking of myself before I thought of the family.

"Well, we must sew the deal up tight before they change their mind," she said. "Can you talk to them about the horse, and Linda, she's good at selling horses. Get the money in the bank before they see something else they like. Thank goodness Mark isn't here trying to push one of his horses onto them."

I looked at Mummy in surprise. She seemed to have become rather worldly. Things really must be desperate in the finance department, and I'd been carrying on with my head in the clouds, just dreaming of my own personal glory.

"I'm going off to bed," I said. I was bone tired. Strong emotions were so exhausting. Not to mention a very long ride to the sea and back. I thought that I would toss and turn all night. My smooth, clean sheets and eiderdown embraced me seductively, and surprisingly, I slept the minute my head touched the pillow.

I woke the next morning, and the events of the previous day flooded back. Carefully, I turned it all over in my mind. Perhaps, 'sleeping on it' would give me a new perspective. Then, it dawned, bright and frighteningly clearly. We were in dire financial straits, and I was the one who could pull us clear. We *had* to sell Skydiver. I began to fear that I had messed it up the day before. Although knowing Jack's character, the fact that I didn't want to sell Skydiver would just egg him on.

I jumped out of bed and slipped into my smartest everyday riding gear. I needed to present myself in the best possible light today. I rushed downstairs and found only Lettie and Rennie deep in conversation over a morning cup of tea. The sideboard hadn't yet been loaded with hot dishes.

"How are you this morning?" I asked cheerfully. "What's on the agenda today?"

"It's our second last day, and it's a cross-country competition organised by John," said Lettie.

"Gosh, John doesn't normally get involved in jumping competitions," I exclaimed, thinking that I had been so caught up in my own affairs that I was not paying attention.

"Well, we don't have enough people to be jump judges, so we're doing a shortened course," explained Rennie.

"What level are we all jumping at?" I asked.

"I think we pick for ourselves, whether it is the lowest, the medium or the highest," said Lettie. "That's what we were discussing. Rennie is on Copperplate, and I'm on Martini, and we thought we would both go for medium."

I poured myself a cup of tea and began to think about it. Normally I would have jumped Balius. I wondered if Jack, Yola and Frank would be taking part. We would have to mount them. Presumably, the use of our horses would go on their bill. I wondered just how much money was in Yola's bank account. I decided to shoot over to the stables and catch up with what was happening today. I suddenly felt a desperate need to know everything that was going on. Also, I would have to tell them that I was willing to sell Skydiver. Put everyone's mind at rest.

Surprisingly, there was no one in the yard. The horses were all neighing their heads off and banging on their doors. That was strange. Neither Linda, Hugh, nor John was there. It was very odd. I hurried into the feed room, and going off the chart on the wall, I mixed up the morning feeds. I did the rounds tipping half-buckets into each of their feed dishes. Then, I filled up all the water buckets. Next was mucking out. I realised, to my deep shame, that I had done absolutely no mucking out since I had got back from Australia. I firmly resolved to get myself back into the swing of things.

Linda and Hugh rushed into the yard as I began on Balius's stable.

"Oh, Jill! We're so sorry! We slept in. John has gone over to fetch Arleen as she's going to help with the jump judging today. It's all hands on deck."

Of course, John had a girlfriend, Arleen. She was artistic and had helped design the brochure for the stables.

"I'm sorry I kicked off yesterday," I told them. "I had no idea that there was a chance of selling Skydiver, and the fact that it was Jack Laskey set me off."

"What's wrong with Jack Laskey?" asked Hugh curiously.

"What's right with him?" I countered darkly. "Anyway, that's not the point, I'm willing to sell Skydiver, and I'll give some of the money to Mummy and Richard and kick some into the pot for the stables so we can be operating with some money in the bank."

Hugh and Linda sighed together. They must have been as worried as Mummy and Richard. That was probably why they had slept in after a sleepless night.

"Yoo-hoo!" called Susan, rushing into the yard, followed by Charles, Janet and Patrick. "We're here to muck out for you this morning. It's our thank you for the wonderful two weeks, so you go and have some breakfast."

"I think I'm due to do some of the work as well," I chirped. "You two go inside. You deserve it."

"No. Jill, you can do your bit soon, but this morning, we've got to sit down and work out who is riding which horse," said Linda, giving me a firm look as if there were things we needed to discuss.

"Before we get back to the castle, there is something we want to talk to you about. The lot from the Dower House will be over there eating. We want to try and sell Firestorm to Jack. We think he might be a good horse for him. He's flashy, and it seems our Jack fancies himself as a horseman, so he will be a fitting challenge for him," said Linda.

"Oh yes! Splendid idea! That will wrap it all up nicely. Will we offer him to Jack to ride the cross-country today?" I asked.

"I thought Linda might ride him. Showcase his talents. I imagine that Jack will want what someone else has got. He likes to think that he's scoring something over someone else. So, if he gets the idea that we've got big plans for Firestorm, he's more likely to want him," said Hugh with his mouth turned down in distaste.

"Are you sure you want to jump him, Linda?" I asked.

"Yes. It's a challenge. I'm going to take him around the high jumps. Having had Janet ride him all fortnight, he should be going well," said Linda determinedly. "It'll be worth it if we can get rid of him."

"As long as he doesn't break your neck!" I commented, knowing that this was a real possibility.

"Hello Jack, Yola, Frank," said Hugh in a loud voice, warning us that the three of them were approaching.

"We're just discussing our plans for the day. We're assuming that all three of you would like to be mounted to go in our little cross-country caper," I said in hearty tones.

"Yes, that's right," said Yola. "I'm serious about dressage, but I do love jumping."

'Of course you do,' I thought to myself.

131

"And you, Frank?" asked Linda.

"If there's a spare horse going, I'd love to have a bash," he said with a good-natured grin.

"We made our way into the dining room and helped ourselves to big plates of scrambled eggs, crispy fried bacon, mushrooms, baked beans and toast."

"This is such a traditional English-type breakfast," tweeted Yola.

"What do you have for breakfast in the States?" I asked politely.

"Yoghurt, crumpets, grits, pancakes and maple syrup, that sort of thing," she replied airily.

Linda had produced a notebook and was writing down the names of all the riders and working out who would ride what. She headed up the list with her name and Firestorm. Then, the prize winners would be riding their usual horses, Patrick and Scarlet Pimpernel, Rennie and Copperplate, Lettie and Martini, Susan and Tranquil, Charles and Secret. Then there were five more riders, Janet, Jack, Yola, Frank and me.

"Don't worry about me if there are not enough to go around," I said.

"No, if we use Bonnie and Jester, there'll be a mount for everyone," she said.

"Yola can have Bonnie, she's certainly reliable, and she could jump that cross-country course blindfold," I said quietly, thinking that we wanted Yola to survive the day unharmed if she were to buy Skydiver.

"She might not think she's flash enough," muttered Hugh.

"No, I think we'll put her on Bonnie, just to be sure," said Linda.

"Do you mind if we put Jack on Balius?" she asked me.

Of course, I minded very much. He was already appropriating Skydiver and now my precious Balius, who I loved from the bottom of my heart. But no other horse I could think of would suit him.

"I suppose so," I agreed reluctantly. "What about Frank?"

"He could ride Jester. He's a reliable old chap, and with a good rider, he certainly ups his game. That would leave you Cammie. Or if you like, you could take Shadow around and just pop him over the odd small jump, give him some more experience."

"Alright, I'll take Shadow," I said. "He went pretty well around the cross-country a few days ago. The more experience he gets, the better."

"Hang on a minute. We've forgotten Janet. Who can we put her on?" said Linda, frowning at the list.

"Well, I suppose she can ride Cammie," said Hugh. "I don't think she'll mind. Any horse has got to be better than Firestorm."

"Ain't that the truth," said Linda quietly.

It looked like today was going to be fun. With the secret plan of luring Jack into buying Firestorm, there was an agreeable note of intrigue.

Chapter Twenty

After breakfast, we trooped down to the stables and found everything mucked out and perfect.

"You lot get over and have your breakfast, and we'll get the horses ready," said Hugh.

John and Arleen drove into the yard.

"We're going to put the numbers and the flags up now," said John.

"We'll saddle up," I said.

"I don't suppose that Skydiver can jump?" suggested Jack, standing too close to me.

"We try not to risk his legs, him being such a good dressage horse," I said, not wanting to let on that Skydiver was also a brilliant jumper. If they bought him, they could find out after they'd paid for him. "We thought you could ride Balius today. You remember that I rode him when I was at Porlock, and we went away to the dressage competition together."

"You make it sound like an assignation," he said, smiling slyly.

Of course, I had thought it was something like that at the time, but he had virtually ignored me the whole time, and it had become evident that the ride on Skydiver was all he had been after.

"You've been wanting to get your hands on Skydiver ever since," I said boldly, throwing caution to the wind, fixing him with a glittering eye.

"Well, is that going to happen? I gathered that you weren't keen," he said, staring me straight in the eyes.

"For that money, you could have me thrown in as well," I said lightly, determined that I would carry it off.

"Really!" he said.

This man was impossible. I shuddered. To think that, at one point, I had been infatuated. Poor, poor Yola!

"Is it a serious offer?" I asked.

"Yes, deadly serious. Yola has her heart set on him."

"Well, we can't deny Yola whatever she wants," I replied dryly. "Put the money in the bank, and he's yours."

"Yola can ring her banker tonight, and they'll arrange the transfer," he replied.

"That's a deal then," I said, hoping that Yola wouldn't break her neck on the course today.

"And you and me?" said Jack with a sly grin. I threw him a look that could curdle cream and flounced off like a panther to whom an indecent suggestion has been made by an alley cat of no breeding.

John came back into the yard. He had drawn out the course on a piece of paper, and he passed it around to each of us to have a look. There was the first jump, the easy pile of logs, then the post-and-rails with the ditch in front, then we avoided the Vicarage Vee and slid straight down the Normandy bank, followed by the Sunken Road, the Barrels and the Garden Seat. We missed the narrow stile into the copse, and went straight on to the tree trunk and, lastly, the Picture Frame.

"Once you've had a look at the piece of paper, I thought we might all walk it together," announced John.

I was glad that the two hardest jumps, the Vicarage Vee and the narrow stile, were missed out. We had to make sure that Linda survived on Firestorm.

"Come on! Let's go!" called John, leading the way. Arleen followed him. Mummy and Richard appeared and brought up the rear. Each had pads, pencils, and little folding stools, so they could be jump judges.

"Ok, this is easy, the logs. Now, while Catherine and Richard are here, let's make a list of who is jumping in which order and which level of jumps each of you is going to choose," said John.

"That will help us as judges," said Mummy.

"Arleen and I will be at the start and the finish, and we're going to time everyone. I expect there'll be a lot of clear rounds so that the fastest time will win," said John. "We can see the log pile, the post-and-rails, and then the last jumps, the tree trunk and the Picture Frame from that vantage point. Then Catherine, if you can be over there to do the Normandy Bank, the Sunken Road, and Richard, the Barrels and the Garden Seat."

"Now, what order?" asked Linda. "I think the riders going for high level first, that's me on Firestorm, then Jack on Balius. Any others for the high level?"

"I think I'll have a go," Patrick said.

"I want to try the highest level, too," said Susan.

"What about me?" whined Yola.

"I think you'll be best going for the middle-level, followed by Frank and Jester, middle level, Lettie and Martini, middle level, Rennie and Copperplate," said Linda.

Yola pouted but said nothing.

"Janet, you're on Cammie, and she's not a very athletic jumper, so if you don't mind the lowest level, Charles on Secret at the lowest level and Jill on Shadow."

"Yes, I think I've got that," said Mummy. "Here, look at this, Linda. Have I got it right? I'll make a copy for John and another for Richard."

"Right, well, let's walk the course, and everyone must remember which jump height they're aiming at," said John.

We followed in a ragged group.

"Perhaps each of you at the different levels should bunch together and discuss approaches," said John.

Thus, Linda, Jack, Patrick, and Susan were walking together in the highest-level group. Jack hadn't yet had a chance to watch Firestorm, but he was curious and was asking Linda about him.

"Oh, yes, we've got big plans for him," said Linda, looking as innocent as if butter wouldn't melt in her mouth. "Mark Lansdowne used to own him. You'd know about him, of course. Unfortunately, Mark couldn't manage him after he had a fall at Burghley, so he passed him on to us for quite a sum of money. We've done a lot of work with him, and Janet, who works for Mr Thorneycroft, he's on the long list for the British eventing team, has been schooling him for us."

Jack narrowed his eyes. I watched in amazement. Linda's artless spiel was working its magic. The arrow went right to the bull's eye.

"He's an impressive-looking animal," said Jack, with an acquisitive gleam in his eye. He must have already walked around the stables assessing each animal. Undoubtedly, he imagined what a dash he would cut mounted on such an animal.

The middle-level group of jumpers were Yola, Lettie, Rennie and Frank. Frank was bright-eyed and bushy-tailed. It was the first time he had walked this course, and he obviously took his trainer responsibilities seriously and discussed each jump with Yola, pointing out angles and the line one would take upon landing.

Our group of low-level jumpers had been around this course several times and joked and pranced about. We were in high spirits. I was excited at the thought of Jack buying Firestorm, and my pulse was racing.

We were each to jump our rounds individually. There were so few of us that there was no need to send off another competitor while the one before was still jumping.

Linda and Firestorm were the first to go. They leapt the high pile of logs as if they were nothing, and she let him gallop on strongly towards the post-and-rails. It was a sizeable jump, and Firestorm paid attention and leapt it judiciously, neither too low nor too high. Firestorm had certainly improved. His performance was more polished and accurate. Linda had such finesse. She harnessed his wild, rebellious spirit and channelled it into the task at hand.

They slid down the Normandy Bank with Linda leaning back and Firestorm's hocks well under his body. They jumped neatly down into the Sunken Road, one tremendous bound and a powerful leap up the other side. The Barrels and the Garden Seat were negotiated successfully, and they were over the substantial end of the tree trunk, neatly through the Picture Frame and galloped through the finish. No matter how well Balius jumped with Jack, I doubted that they would beat that time.

"What was their time?" I asked John.

"Wait until the end," he replied.

Jack set off with a flourish. Balius was going too fast for my liking. He was galloping out of his stride and had to leap high and wide to make it over the log pile. I was proud of him when I saw him steady himself, despite Jack's determined efforts to push him on. My gallant horse stumbled a little at the bottom of the slide but managed to regain his balance to jump down into the Sunken Road, two strides, and up the other side. I crossed my fingers, hoping that Jack wouldn't bring down one of my favourite horses. It was better that he never knew that Skydiver could jump. The last four jumps were easy for Balius, who had jumped them a hundred times. Jack pushed him very hard, but there was no way he would be quicker than Linda. They got through the finish, and he didn't even pat Balius, who was heaving. He jumped off and looked around for someone to take the reins. He was a despicable pig, and I swore that was the last time he ever got on Balius, no matter how much money he paid.

Patrick set off on the lanky Scarlet Pimpernel. He rode very well, sitting in a correct position, finding the horse's rhythm and placing him carefully in front of each jump. I hoped that he would do well with Archer. He came galloping through the finish in a low-key way. He wasn't determined to prove himself to anyone. Susan and Tranquil were a funny pair. They were both laidback and relaxed, but today they seemed rather energised. All of Susan's years of instruction from Major Holbrooke were in evidence. They did a copybook round, and Tranquil's long legs seemed to eat up the miles. I suspected that they would be second.

Then Yola galloped up, her arms and legs waving like windmills. She was probably peeved that she'd been given Bonnie, who, to an American not used to cobs, did have the appearance of a small draught horse. Bonnie didn't care. Being an old hand, who had experienced many different types of riders, she galloped on steadily. Yola was careless and didn't ride accurately, and after the post-and-rails, Bonnie headed for the Vicarage Vee, where she jumped expertly. This was the normal course that she had followed so many times. We all watched with concern, but Yola didn't notice that she'd gone off-piste. Then, she pulled up and looked around, unable to work out where the next jump was.

"You're disqualified. Wrong course!" Richard yelled out to her.

She scowled and rode back to the start.

"What was that about?"

"Number three was the Normandy Bank. Look at the numbers. You weren't meant to jump the Vicarage Vee," I said quietly.

"I don't understand these darn stupid names for jumps. This stupid plug took me the wrong way," she cried.

"I don't think Bonnie is meant to read the numbers for you," I retorted.

"My fault Yola. I should have gone over the course with you more accurately," said Frank tactfully. Then, he set off on Jester.

"Good luck!" I called. He gave me a big, confident grin.

Jester looked interested. It wasn't often that he was ridden in a cross-country course, and he entered into the spirit of it. They went around clear, and I realised that Frank really was a competent rider in a non-showy, quiet way. Lettie galloped around at a very fast speed on little Martini, who had the same courage and skill as her young rider. Rennie rode carefully, thinking more of Copperplate's welfare than a fast time.

Janet was the next one to go. Her long legs hung down Cammie's rotund sides.

"Come on, you lazy creature," she said kindly.

Cammie tossed her pretty head and deigned to canter neatly towards the lowest pile of logs. They proceeded around the course quietly at a slow hand gallop. Then, it was Charles' turn on Secret. He was obviously feeling competitive. Secret loved jumping, and she had taken to cross-country like a duck to water.

He came in very fast. I set off on Shadow. As it was only a training round, I trotted up to the pile of logs, cantered around the post-and-rails, and we slid down the bank. I skipped the Sunken Road, but we cantered over the Barrels, the Garden Seat, and the tree trunk and hopped neatly through the Picture Frame.

"You didn't do the proper course," Jack scoffed at me, his hands on his hips.

I refused to answer. It was none of his business.

"Let's go into lunch, and we'll announce the results," said John.

We rode back to the stables. I led Balius from Shadow, and Frank dismounted and led Jester and Bonnie.

Jack and Yola stalked on ahead of us, deep in whispered conversation. They were probably saying that Yola should have been given a better horse than Bonnie. Or, hopefully, they were plotting to buy Firestorm.

Lunch felt like a festive occasion. There were sandwiches, slices of egg and potato pie, a cheese board, bowls of fruit, and trifle.

John stood up and asked for silence.

"Fastest round over the high jumps, Linda and Firestorm, followed by Susan and Tranquil, Jack and Balius and Patrick on Scarlet Pimpernel."

Linda smiled modestly, Susan beamed, and Jack looked thunderous.

"The middle jumps were first Lettie, second Rennie and third Frank. The lower jumps were first by several seconds Charles, and second Janet."

Everyone, except Jack and Yola, clapped and yodelled and shouted hurray. We were in roaring good spirits, and the room bubbled with joyous revelry.

"We must talk to you," Jack said to Linda.

"Yes, how can I help?" she replied smoothly.

"It's about Firestorm," he went on.

"Alright, then this is a discussion with me, Hugh, Jill and John," she replied.

"How much for the big chestnut gelding?" he asked bluntly.

He couldn't even remember his name. He deserved Firestorm more than anyone else I could think of.

"I'm sure Firestorm will suit you very well, Jack. While Yola is mastering the fine arts of *haute école,* you can be out there storming around Badminton and Burghley. I must admit he is a man's horse."

I thought she was laying it on with a trowel, but Jack's egotistical nature blinded him. He was smiling like that cat who had got the Chantilly cream, licking his lips, impatient to know the price.

"We'd be prepared to give you Firestorm for just £5,000 since you're paying such a handsome price for Skydiver," said Linda, as if she were bestowing an enormous treat upon him.

"That's a deal then," he said. I wondered if he would have paid more.

"Shall I get Hugh to draw up the sales agreements? I assume that you'll have them checked by a vet?"

"I don't think that will be necessary," said Jack. "Let's do the paperwork, sign on the dotted line and Yola can ring her banker tonight."

I admired Linda's approach to business. She was so smooth, unassuming and apparently guileless, a brilliant business woman. I realised then just how much of a gem we had in her.

Chapter Twenty-One

"What shall we do for your last day?" I asked the prize winners.

They looked at each other.

"A ride around the loch?" suggested Charles.

"Another spin around the cross-country?" asked Patrick, perhaps thinking he would ride Archer.

"I thought I might bring the three ex-racehorses in and give them some schooling," said Linda. "If any of you would like to ride them, you would be very welcome."

"That sounds fun," said Charles, determined to show his beloved what a fun, brave person he was.

"Training an ex-racehorse is rather different to breaking in a horse from scratch. You can put a saddle on them and ride them, but their old bad habits need to be broken."

The three thoroughbreds were a wild-looking bunch. They'd hardly been ridden since they'd come up to Blainstock. There was a rangy chestnut mare with very large ears and a tendency to paddle with her front feet, swinging her legs outward in a slightly circular movement, but with no danger of hitting herself. A nondescript, anxious, brown gelding with scrawny haunches, and a bay gelding, standing over 16.2 hh with good conformation.

"The bay is called Rumble, and he's certainly the pick of the bunch," said Linda. "The other two aren't much, but I thought we could do something with them to give them a second chance at life, otherwise, they would have gone for meat."

"Oh no!" exclaimed soft-hearted Susan.

"What are their names?" asked Rennie, who liked to keep everything clear in her head. She was vaguely thinking that the chestnut mare might suit Miss Brandon at the riding school. There was something about her.

"The chestnut mare is Vanity, and the brown gelding is Chocolate. Now! Let's get down to business."

"Can I ride Vanity?" asked Rennie. Linda looked at her in surprise. Rennie was normally so timid and never put herself forward.

"Of course, you can," she agreed. "Who wants Chocolate?"

"I'll have a go," said Charles, who was determined to garner as many new experiences as possible.

"And the handsome Rumble?" said Linda.

No one stepped forward. Then, Janet hesitantly raised her hand.

"If no one else wants a go, I'll ride him," she said.

"Good-oh," said Linda. "Mount up, everyone."

The three horses walked on the right rein around the perimeter of the school. Susan, Lettie and I sat on the seat to watch. Linda stood in the middle of the arena.

"I want you all riding on a loose rein. Don't worry about Chocolate rushing forward, Charles. Bring him back to the walk and give him a long rein until he begins to understand that it isn't a race."

Charles had gone red in the face, trying to restrain Chocolate, who was all stirred up. Janet sat confidently on Rumble and persuaded him to walk out well. He certainly looked promising, and I wondered whether he might not be a good competition prospect for Linda. Rennie was sitting quietly on Vanity, who walked carefully as if treading on eggshells.

"Now, I want you to ride on a relatively long rein, with just a spider touch on the mouth. If you feel them rushing forward, try a half-halt, taking up a momentary pressure on their mouths and then releasing. Trot on."

Chocolate tossed his head in the air and went to rush forward. Charles grabbed at the reins and then remembered the instructions. Rumble and Vanity trotted on, their heads high, noses stuck out in the air.

"Lengthen those reins and let them find their own balance. Spectators, would you mind putting some poles on the ground down the centre of the arena, three big steps between each pole."

Once eight poles were laid on the ground, the horses turned at the far end and trotted over them. There was some stumbling and shortened strides and leaps until they got into the rhythm of it.

"Change the rein and trot around the other way and then up the middle again," said Linda.

It was repetitive, and soon the horses settled and managed to stride over the poles.

"Rennie, you're doing well with Vanity. You two seem to get on," said Linda. "Now, walk. Helpers, please take away the poles. The next exercise is turn on the forehand, and to make it easier, I want a helper on each horse. We want to teach them to move away from a leg. Halt on the long side, and then the helpers push them around, pivoting on their forelegs. As you push, the rider uses their legs. Shouldn't take them long to learn."

All the horses managed to pivot around several times.

"I think that's enough for now. The next lesson they will learn will be leg yielding. But now, to help them relax, walk out up the path between the fields to the top when you look down on the loch, and then turn around and bring them back. Then we'll give them each a dipperful of corn and they can go back into the field."

"That was uneventful," said Susan.

"As all good training should be," replied Linda primly.

"I suppose you all need to pack this afternoon," I told them at lunch.

"It will be so sad to leave," wailed Susan.

The others agreed.

"Jill," said Rennie after lunch, staring into my face intently when the others rose and left the table. "I really, really like Vanity, and I was wondering if she might be for sale."

I was surprised.

"I have to talk to the others, but what do you want to do with her?" I asked.

"I thought I might be able to train her for myself," she replied. "I don't have much money but Dad and Miss Brandon might help me to pay for her, depending on whether she is expensive."

I went and talked to the others at the stables.

"I think it's a good match," said Linda, as if they were getting married. "We didn't pay much for her. She's pretty ordinary. I think we just add an extra £30 to her cost price, and we let Rennie pay her off as she can afford it. Hopefully, the magazine will let her share a truck and drop her off when they take one of the other horses."

"Done deal," said John. "I like that Rennie. She deserves a break."

I went to tell Rennie. She was ecstatic.

"Oh! Jill! Thank you so much. I promise I will do my very best for her and pay you as quickly as possible."

"Don't worry about it," I replied. "Just when you can afford it. We've sold two horses this week, and we're sharing the love."

The following day the prize winners packed up their luggage, which was loaded and the horses, plus Archer and Vanity. Away they went.

"Now you've got a spare moment; I want to show you something I've been working on," said Mummy.

I followed her up to the library.

"We were getting desperate about the money, so I thought I would return to my former profession, but with a difference. It was Hamish who gave me the idea. I've written a children's book for much younger children."

She handed me some sheets of paper.

"These illustrations are gorgeous," I exclaimed. "That pony looks like a small version of Black Boy."

"Yes," she replied. "It is a good likeness."

"But surely you haven't become an artist?"

"No, it was Arleen. You know. John's girlfriend."

"Goodness, These are so good. Is a publisher interested?"

"I've got to send them down to London, now they're finished. My agent is excited about it."

"So, the dance moves on," I said philosophically.

"Your own life might be taking a rather different turn," said Mummy, with a knowing glance.

On Monday morning, the castle was very quiet, like being inside an Egyptian pyramid. Mummy, Richard and I sat together at the breakfast table and looked at each other.

"Are we expecting our tenants for breakfast?" asked Richard.

"Cook sent over some supplies, so they're fixing their own this morning," said Mummy.

Richard smiled.

"Well, I think the prize winners thing went very well," said Mummy. "We managed the hospitality side. They were a jolly bunch. It was good for Jill to have some young people around."

"You're talking about me as if I'm not here," I commented.

"It's fun having guests and even better when they leave," said Richard.

As he said this, Frank popped his head in and coughed discreetly.

"I'm sorry to interrupt," he began politely.

"Not at all, dear," said Mummy. "Come and sit down and share our breakfast, or at least a cup of tea."

Frank pulled up a chair, and Mummy poured him a cup of tea.

"Could I ask a favour," he began. "I thought I might go into Kilkarny and do some shopping today, and I wondered if you might lend me a vehicle. Jack and Yola are taking the rented car to Aberdeen to arrange our own transport and open bank accounts."

"Of course, of course," said Richard amiably. "You can take the Land Rover, and Jill could perhaps go with you, show you the way."

I almost glared at him, thinking he was setting us up, but caught myself in time. I was determined to return to my youthful easy-go-lucky character after my recent spate of bad behaviour over Skydiver. But, I was feeling spiky when it came to Frank.

"We did have an incident this morning, so top of the list is rat poison," said Frank.

"An incident?" echoed Mummy.

"It's really not the done thing to poison your employers," I said reprovingly. "Who would pay your wages?"

Everyone laughed uneasily. I wondered if I might write a book, *Murder at Blainstock Castle*.

"Yola slipped her angel feet into her slippers, and it seemed that a sweet little rodent, having been recently evicted, had nested there and produced a brood of pink, blind, hairless babies," recounted Frank.

We chortled collectively.

"Oh, that is priceless!" I gasped.

"She did rather carry on. Our Yola is not one to take things quietly," said Frank, with an air of resigned experience. "So, I'm off to pick up rat poison, food supplies, and a collection of useful items such as candles, matches, soap powder, detergent, and anything else that a well-supplied house should have."

"You will definitely need Jill to help carry the goods," said Mummy, with wide-open innocent eyes. She made it sound like I was a packhorse.

Thus, Frank and I set out for Kilkarny. I drove the Land Rover. We were on a mission. There is something rather intimate about travelling in a vehicle together. There is no need to look at each other, no way of getting away from the conversation for the length of the drive, and it creates an atmosphere conducive for confidences. I intended to take the opportunity to grill Frank on the circumstances of the Laskey marriage.

In all the cut and thrust that had been going on since Jack Laskey had landed with his wife at Blainstock, Frank and I had not had a moment alone. The prize winners had left. It was time that we talked.

I had written to Frank several times when he had been in America, since I had last seen him, on that fateful night last summer, that he had taken me out for a pizza. The first letter I had sent from Chatton before I left for Australia. Then I had written again from Australia, but hadn't mentioned anything about meeting my father. That was too big and far too personal to commit to paper.

Now was a perfect opportunity to find out about the saga with Jack and Lola. What had happened to Jack's engagement to Willow and his entanglement with Belinda Bliss? Were they actually married, or had they run away together like Lydia and Wickham? Although in this case, Yola was hardly penniless! It was sure to be a tawdry tale, but that made it all the more fascinating.

I was wary of talking to Frank about Jack. I hated the idea that Jack might have boasted that I had been infatuated with him, and that was how he had come to ride Skydiver at the dressage test. I would just have to brazen it out. Frank was too much of a gentleman to say anything, even if he did suspect.

"Did you know Jack and Yola before they married?" I asked, trying an oblique approach.

Frank grinned at me.

"You want to know whether or not they're really married?" he queried, one eyebrow raised quizzically.

I stared at him. Obviously, I was underestimating his insight.

"Yes, I knew both of them, vaguely. Then, I sort of got caught up in their courtship, which was difficult."

"Did you know Willow Vetch?" I asked.

"Yes, and when I met Jack, he was engaged to Willow, and Belinda Bliss was swanning about mixing it up," he replied.

"So, Jack broke it off with Willow when he was sure that he could snag Yola?" I hazarded a guess.

"Uh huh," nodded Frank. "You've obviously divined the character of Jack," he said and laughed.

"The nicest way to put it is he's a Jack the Lad," I quipped.

"And then some," he added. "But don't underestimate Yola. She was a big driver in this situation. Determined to have him."

"Throwing Willow over is reminiscent of an early Victorian melodrama. I understand that her father Bernard Vetch is a force to be reckoned with. He manufactures arms and sells them to both sides in any war. It makes for better business."

"I think the wrath of an arms manufacturer might be easier to deal with than Belinda Bliss's fury," said Frank wryly.

"Poor Willow, she was a lost soul," I said.

"Not our Yola. What Yola wants, Yola gets. Unfortunately, her American family are more class conscious than anything our fusty old aristocracy can come up with. They harken back to the Gilded Age. The shame of Yola running off with someone else's fiancé has cast a cloud upon the whole family. She is only nineteen, but under the terms of her family trust, she inherits all her fortune when she marries, which means that she and Jack have squillions to splash around. They decided to escape across the Atlantic until the scandal blows over."

"Now, I'm getting the picture. So, paying exorbitant prices for Skydiver and Firestorm won't break the bank," I sighed with relief.

"They could probably buy Blainstock Castle ten times over," said Frank.

"It's not for sale," I retorted, suddenly feeling very loyal to our family home.

"How come you got to be hired by them?" I asked.

"It's a bit complicated, but I left my job in Virginia to come over here with Jack and Yola," he replied evasively. "You must tell me all about Australia. I thought it might be rather fun to go over there for a while."

Immediately my mind scampered along a ridiculous line of thought completely off the track of any sensible logic. Perhaps after we married, we might go there on our honeymoon, and we could spend some time with my father riding brumbies in the mountains. So, you can see, dear readers, that I was, to say the very least, jumping the gun. But I defy any woman of marriageable age to deny that they immediately think about walking down the aisle when surveying a decent prospective husband who is showing interest. It is just what we do.

I quickly banished the idea.

"Let's make a list of everything one could possibly need to run a house," I said. "We can talk about Australia later."

We spent a good day in Kilkarny, shopping for food and buying up half of the goods in the hardware store.

We got back. Mummy and Richard told me that the £25,000 was now safely in the Blainstock account. I told them what I had decided. I wanted to give £8,000 to them and £8,000 into the bank account of the stables, and £4,000 for myself, tucked away for a rainy day. It was a double bubble celebration, and the gloomy skies cleared, and we could plan. My golden summer in Oxfordshire was shimmering on the horizon. But now, Frank was in Scotland, and that did make a difference.

"That is not the only good news," said Mummy. "Ann rang up this morning, and she and Henry were setting off to come up here for several days. She fancies a short holiday before she knuckles down and studies non-stop for her final exams."

Ann has been my best friend since we were tots, and Henry is her faithful boyfriend, a vet.

"Oh, that is wonderful!" I enthused. "And Henry has never been here. We'll be able to go riding all day, to the sea, school in the arena, jump around the cross-country course."

"Yes, and they can catch up with Frank as well. He's one of the Chatton crowd, isn't he?" said Mummy. "She's going to ring when they're just a few hours away."

The next day after lunch, Ann and Henry arrived just after Yola and Jack swept up the drive, each driving a brand spanking new vehicle, Yola the latest Land Rover and Jack a shiny red sports car. Frank hurried off to help his employers unpack their shopping bags, and Mummy and I ushered in Ann and Henry.

"You can't imagine how happy I am to see you," I told Ann, who was going to share my turret room at the top of the castle. Henry was to sleep in the blue guest room.

"You've got so much to tell me. Australia! Everything that happened. And your mother told me that Frank Stabley is here with an American couple. He's their horse trainer? How on earth did that come about?"

"I can't even begin to tell all right now. We have to go down and join the others for drinks and then dinner. I'll just briefly explain about Jack and Lola Laskey. I met him when he was an instructor at Porlock Vale.

"I remember you talking about him," interjected Ann. I kept going.

"He rode Skydiver in a dressage competition for me, and he did fancy him. Then he was engaged to a weird girl called Willow with a very lascivious guardian, Belinda Bliss."

"No one has a surname – Bliss!" exclaimed Ann.

"Yes, they do, and it certainly suits her, not to mention alliterative."

"Anyway, he broke it off with Willow and ran off with Lola. Her family don't approve, and they've rented the Dower House, and they're lying low. Lola is immensely rich, and they've bought Skydiver for the astronomical price of £20,000 and also another horse called Firestorm for £5,000. Basically, it saved our bacon as we were on the verge of insolvency. Frank told them about this place, and they've hired him as their horse trainer, but he does all sorts of jobs for them."

Ann was uncharacteristically silent. Her mouth gaped open in astonishment.

"That's only half of it!" I said. "But we must be on our best behaviour tonight. Yola and Jack, and Frank are coming to dinner. They're our best customers, and we have to treat them with respect, even though Jack and Yola are the absolute pits. Of course, Frank isn't."

"No, he's always been a decent sort," agreed Ann.

Dinner went off well. Ann was very good socially, and Henry had impeccable manners. Jack and Yola were full of their own news - the cars they had purchased, not to mention the story of the mouse and its babies in Yola's slipper.

"Tomorrow, you're to ride Firestorm, and we're all coming to watch," I said to Jack. I was looking forward to that. Although it wouldn't do our business much good if Jack was deposited on his behind, it would be very satisfying to watch.

"Can we all go riding tomorrow," piped up Ann.

"Of course," I said. "You and Henry can have the pick of all the horses in the stable, and we can go up into the hills or jump around the cross-country course."

When we went to bed, Ann and I talked long into the night about meeting my father in Australia. I was going to speak to her about Frank but thought it might wait until the next bedtime chat.

Chapter Twenty-Two

After breakfast, we all went over to the indoor school to watch Jack ride Firestorm. I was very curious to see how the two of them would get on. I knew that Linda was thankful that she was never going to have to ride the chestnut monster again. If Jack wasn't around and Firestorm needed exercise, he could be let out in the field or lunged.

"He is a magnificent looking animal," said Ann admiringly as John led him over. Indeed, Firestorm was impressive. His personality was as grand as his good looks. His muscles rippled beneath his satiny bright gold coat. His long mane and tail swirled as John ran him up and down in front of us.

Jack stood in the centre of the arena, fiddling with the very expensive-looking gold watch on his wrist.

John brought him over. Firestorm arched his neck extravagantly and mouthed his bit.

"He's a showy horse," said Henry.

"He goes best when you ride him every step of the way. He has to be told what to do, or his brain fizzes over with his own self-importance," said Linda to Jack. Then, she came over to sit with us. Frank and Yola joined us.

"This should be interesting," I said as Jack mounted. Yola threw me a sharp look, and I shut up.

Jack mounted, then they walked to the end of the arena and turned left, down the long side, close to the wall. Firestorm was quickstepping with small, jerky steps, his head high, his jaw set. Jack didn't look fazed. After one circuit of the arena, he pushed him into a trot. Firestorm was snorting, flinging his hoofs out in a wild, extravagant movement, rolling his eyes and swishing his tail. He was displaying all the warning behaviours of a horse which is ill at ease. Jack took a tighter hold on the reins, closed his legs, and they were cantering in a wild, rollicking gait. Lola was watching wide-eyed, twisting her hands in her lap.

Jack sat down in the saddle, braced his back, closed his legs and took a firm hold on the reins, and Firestorm came back to a walk. Then, he halted, a four-square halt. Jack asked him to walk forward on a loose rein, and he relaxed. The psychic tension in the air dissolved. Firestorm seemed to have decided that Jack was alright. Only a twisted maniac of a horse could have come to such a conclusion!

Jack rode back over.

"I think this horse and I are going to do very well together. What do you think, sweetness?" he asked Yola.

"Whatever you think, Jack," replied Yola.

Yola had a dressage lesson with Linda, and Jack was going to watch. This left Frank free to come riding with us.

We had a wonderful day, just the four of us, perfectly attuned to each other. Ann rode Copperplate, Henry on Balius, Frank on Rumble and me on Shadow. We took it quietly due to Rumble and Shadow, still in the early stages of training.

We chattered on about all our friends in Chatton, and I was swept with homesickness. As beautiful as were the Scottish Highlands, Oxfordshire had been my childhood home. Frank was planning to go down and see his parents for a week or two, as soon as Jack and Yola were settled in the Dower House.

"Would you like to come with me Jill?" he asked.

I went bright red. I wasn't sure exactly what he meant. He looked at me expectantly. Was he asking me to go and meet his parents? Or was he thinking that I might just like to go south to catch up with my Chattonite friends?

"I'll think about it," I muttered, feeling my face go hot and red.

That night Ann and I climbed the stairs to my turret room. Ann had declared herself exhausted by all the fresh air.

"Jillikins," she said to me sternly as we snuggled into our beds. "You absolutely have to tell me what is going on between you and Frank. You're in love, aren't you? Has he declared himself? He looks at you with cow's eyes. He's obviously totally smitten."

"I don't know what you're talking about," I retorted. "You know I've never been one to be the least bit paralysed with a longing for love. I've never indulged in unrequited, impossibly delicious passions for men who wouldn't recognise me if I walked past them in the street. I never fantasised about attending a ball and dancing, floating on a cloud, pressed by a manly arm to a manly breast."

"That might be so," said Ann, "but that's not exactly what I asked. We're not talking about imaginary passions for unknown men. We're talking about Frank. You've even had a date with him. I bet you exchanged letters while you were away, didn't you?"

"Yes," I admitted.

151

"So, there you go. You're experiencing the strangest feeling, overwhelming and exhilarating at the same time. An uncontrollable force. You can't look at him without fear or embarrassment."

"Well, there might be something like that."

Ann sat up in bed and turned on the lamp, staring at me.

"Jillikins, you're a dill. For someone so smart, you can be such a clot."

"What does that mean?" I asked hotly.

"It means that you totally underestimated 'being in love'. It is real and truly terrific. Finally!"

"So, you and Henry have got that as well then?" I asked doubtfully. Somehow, I had thought that no one else in the world had experienced what I had when I was with Frank.

"Yes," said Ann.

"Gosh!" I exclaimed as waves of awareness and revelation swept over me. I felt like I was drowning in a new form of knowingness. It seemed that I was now one of the initiated. I foresaw tremendous chats between Ann and myself regarding this new realm of experience. Everything had suddenly become clear. But nothing had been spoken between Frank and myself.

"You have to wait for him to declare himself," said Ann. "Don't jump the gun. Let him lead the situation."

That was fine with me. But perhaps I would accept his invitation to go down to Chatton.

THE END

BIBLIOGRAPHY

Badger, Jane. *Heroines on Horseback: The Pony Book in Children's Fiction,* first published by Girls Gone By, 2013.

Edwards, Monica. *Rennie Goes Riding,* first published by Collins, 1956, illustrations by Sheila Rose.

Ferguson, Ruby. *Jill's Gymkhana,* first published by Hodder & Stoughton, 1949, illustrations by Caney.

Ferguson, Ruby. *A Stable for Jill,* first published by Hodder & Stoughton, 1951, illustrations by Caney.

Ferguson, Ruby. *Jill Has Two Ponies,* first published by Hodder & Stoughton, 1952, illustrations by Caney.

Ferguson, Ruby. *Jill Enjoys Her Ponies* (renamed *Jill and the Runaway* in 1993), first published by Hodder & Stoughton, 1954, illustrations by Caney.

Ferguson, Ruby. *Jill's Riding Club,* first published by Hodder & Stoughton, 1956, illustrations by Caney.

Ferguson, Ruby. *Rosettes for Jill,* first published by Hodder & Stoughton, 1957, illustrations by Caney.

Ferguson, Ruby. *Jill and the Perfect Pony,* first published by Hodder & Stoughton, 1959, illustrations by Caney.

Ferguson, Ruby. *Pony Jobs for Jill* (renamed *Challenges by Jill* in 1993), first published by Hodder & Stoughton, 1960, illustrations by Caney.

Ferguson, Ruby. *Jill's Pony Trek,* first published by Hodder & Stoughton, 1962, illustrations by Caney.

Pullein Thompson, Diana. *A Pony for Sale,* first published by Collins, 1951, illustrations by Sheila Rose.

Pullein Thompson, Diana. *Janet Must Ride,* first published by Collins, 1953, illustrations by Mary Gernat.

Pullein Thompson, Josephine. *Six Ponies,* first published by Collins, 1946, illustrations by Anne Bullen.

Pullein Thompson, Josephine. *Pony Club Team,* first published by Collins, 1950, illustrations by Sheila Rose.

Pullein Thompson, Josephine. *Prince Among Ponies*, first published by Collins, 1952, illustrations by Charlotte Hough.

Pullein Thompson, Josephine. *One Day Event*, first published by Collins, 1954, illustrations by Sheila Rose.

Pullein Thompson, Josephine. *Showjumping Secret*, first published by Collins, 1955, illustrations by Sheila Rose.

Pullein Thompson, Josephine. *Pony Club Camp*, first published by Collins, 1957, illustrations by Sheila Rose.

Spark, Jemma. *Jill Rides Cross-Country,* published in 2018 by Epona Publishing.

Spark, Jemma. *Jill Has Two Horses*, published in 2018 by Epona Publishing.

Spark, Jemma. *Jill Goes Pony Trekking*, published in 2019 by Epona Publishing.

Spark, Jemma. *Jill and the Steeplechaser*, published in 2020 by Epona Publishing.

Spark, Jemma. *Jill Dreams of a Dressage Horse*, published in 2020 by Epona Publishing.

Spark, Jemma. *Jill and the Horsemasters*, published in 2020 by Epona Publishing.

Spark, Jemma. *All Change at Blainstock Stables: Jill Goes Into Business*, published in 2021 by Epona Publishing.

Spark, Jemma. *Jill's Ponies: Black Boy and Rapide*, published in 2021 by Epona Publishing.

Spark, Jemma. *The Adventures of Jill's Ponies*, published in 2022 by Epona Publishing.